SEASON OF THE WARRIOR

Out of respect, Touch the Sky had refused to desecrate his enemy's flag. But look what they had done to Bear Tooth. He felt no shame when hot tears momentarily filmed his eyes—Little Horse, too, was rapidly blinking back tears.

But the moment passed. Once again Touch the Sky made his heart a stone with no soft places left in it. Thus, it was ready for the hard battle to come, where every soft place would only be one more spot for his enemy to wound.

"If this was meant to make us show the white feather and flee," Little Horse said bitterly, "these Yellow Eyes are confusing the Cheyenne with the Poncas. Fresh white scalps will soon dangle from my clout, brother. I swear this thing."

"More of us will die, too," Touch the Sky said. "More of us will look like Bear Tooth before it is over. But I swear by the direction of the four winds, before we have done with them, these whites will do the hurt dance while we smear our bodies with their blood!"

CHEYENNE
10

BUFFALO
HIDERS
JUDD COLE

LEISURE BOOKS　　**NEW YORK CITY**

A LEISURE BOOK®

June 1994

Published by

Dorchester Publishing Co., Inc.
276 Fifth Avenue
New York, NY 10001

Printed in the United States of America.

Prologue

In 1840, during the Moon When the Ponies Shed, Running Antelope of the Northern Cheyenne led his wife, infant son, and 30 braves on their annual journey to visit their Southern Cheyenne kinsmen living below the Platte River.

They rode under a white flag to show they were at peace. Nonetheless, they were ambushed by blue-bloused pony soldiers near the North Platte. The vastly outnumbered warriors lived up to the legendary name their enemies had given them: the Fighting Cheyenne. But stone war clubs, flint-tipped arrows, and single-shot muzzle-loaders were no match for the Bluecoats' deadly accurate carbines and big-thundering wagon guns. When the smoke finally cleared, Running Antelope, his wife, and all 30 braves lay dead or dying. The only survivor was the infant boy.

His life spared by order of the lieutenant in charge, he was taken back to the river-bend settlement of Bighorn Falls near Fort Bates in the Wyoming Territory. He was adopted by merchant John Hanchon and his barren wife Sarah. They named him Matthew. At first, their love was enough to shelter him from the cruel reality of growing up Indian in a white man's world.

Then came his sixteenth year and his first love—Kristen, daughter of the wealthy rancher Hiram Steele. Suddenly, Matthew's life came all unraveled like a frayed rope. Caught in his secret meeting place with Kristen, he was soundly thrashed by one of Steele's wranglers. Steele threatened to kill him if he ever caught Matthew with Kristen again. Knowing he was as good as dead otherwise, Kristen lied and told him she never wanted to see him again.

That incident loosed an avalanche of trouble. Seth Carlson, a cavalry officer with plans to marry Kristen, delivered an ultimatum to Matthew: Either the Cheyenne left Bighorn Falls for good, or Carlson would ruin his parents' all-important mercantile contract with nearby Fort Bates—the lifeblood of their business.

Caught between the sap and the bark, Matthew hardened his heart, said goodbye to the only life he knew, and rode north toward the upcountry of the Powder River, Cheyenne country. He was soon captured by braves from Chief Yellow Bear's tribe. The tribe Council of Forty declared him a spy and sentenced him to torture and death.

Matthew was tied to a wagon wheel and tortured over flames. Then, as a bitter young junior warrior named Wolf Who Hunts Smiling was about to kill the unconscious youth, old Arrow Keeper intervened.

Arrow Keeper was the tribal shaman and had recently experienced a powerful medicine dream—one that foretold the arrival of a tall young stranger who would bear the mark of the warrior. And Arrow Keeper found that mark buried past the youth's hairline, a mulberry-colored birthmark in the shape of a perfect arrowhead. This was the mysterious stranger of his vision— destined to lead the Cheyenne people in one last, great victory against their enemies.

Arrow Keeper buried the name Matthew in a hole forever and renamed the tall youth Touch the Sky. Honey Eater, daughter of Chief Yellow Bear, was secretly relieved when the handsome newcomer's life was spared. But Black Elk, the fierce young war leader who loved her, was outraged. So were many others, including his wily young cousin Wolf Who Hunts Smiling.

Through sheer determination to belong somewhere, and against incredible odds, Touch the Sky became the best warrior Black Elk ever trained. He saved his village from Pawnee attackers, routed a ruthless gang of whiskey peddlers, prevented land-grabbers from stealing Cheyenne hunting grounds, rescued Cheyenne women and children from their Kiowa-Comanche captors. Such bravery had gradually earned the respect of his loyal blood brother Little Horse and other fellow Cheyennes. But each time he came close to full acceptance, his tribal enemies cleverly revived the old rumor that he was secretly a spy for the hair-faced white men.

Once hard but fair, Black Elk let jealousy over Honey Eater's love for the tall young buck turn his heart to stone—especially now that Honey Eater was his unwilling bride and had not given him a child. Now, like his power-hungry cousin Wolf Who Hunts Smiling, he watched for the first opportunity to kill Touch the Sky.

The youth had finally accepted the destiny foretold in Arrow Keeper's great medicine vision; he had even experienced that vision himself. But he also remembered the old shaman's warning: *First must come many trials and much suffering before you raise high the lance of leadership.*

Chapter One

In the Moon When the Green Grass Is Up, Chief Gray Thunder's Cheyenne band packed their entire camp onto travois.

Facing east, singing the Song to the New Sun Rising, they rode out one morning at dawn from their winter camp in the Tongue River Valley. The warm moons would be spent grazing their winter-starved ponies at their permanent summer camp near the fork of the Powder and the Little Powder. Once the ponies were strong, scouts would be sent out to locate the buffalo herds for the annual hunt.

"Brother!" the sturdy brave named Little Horse said, nudging his pony up beside Touch the Sky's. "The spring runoff has begun, the valleys are no longer locked by ice. The short white days are behind us, and I feel as keen as Brother Bear emerging from his long sleep. Our ponies will grow strong and sleek. *Then* we will ride again and feel the wind in our hair!"

"Buck, I have ears for this. Though its ribs look like bent bows, see how my pony is already trying to sprout wings and fly!"

Touch the Sky had 20 winters behind him. He was lean and straight and tall, with a strong, hawk nose and black eyes. His long hair, dark as his eyes, was cut close above his brows to keep his vision clear. Like his smaller friend, he wore beaded leggings, a soft kid breechclout, elkskin moccasins. A leather band around his left wrist protected it from the slap of his buffalo-sinew bowstring.

The cold moons had been especially long and bitter. The bone-chilling wind howled like mating wolves, forcing Gray Thunder's Cheyenne to keep the fires blazing all night in their lodges. They had passed the long evenings telling stories, sleeping late during the coldest part of the days. Now bright columbine and verbena dotted the plains, and Cheyenne spirits were blossoming with them.

"Sadly," Little Horse said, glancing behind them, "warm weather also lures the snakes from their nests."

Touch the Sky glanced in the same direction, and no further words were necessary. Behind them, riding side by side in the long double column, were Wolf Who Hunts Smiling and his fawning lackey, Swift Canoe.

"Look at Wolf Who Hunts Smiling," Little

Horse added. "See how his eyes dart everywhere? He has grown shifty-eyed from watching for the ever-expected attack. See, even now he points in our direction. Place these words near your heart. All through the short white days, he shed much brain sweat plotting your downfall."

"Truly, it has become a favorite sport with him. Between him and his cousin Black Elk, I have learned to surround my sleeping robes with dried pods."

Even as Touch the Sky spoke, Black Elk turned on his roan pony to glance back. As battle chief, he led the defensive columns of warriors. The women, children, and elders traveled between the columns, the very old and very young lashed to travois.

Touch the Sky watched Black Elk stare at Honey Eater where she rode with the other women of her clan. He averted his own gaze just in time—as he did often now, since Black Elk was trying to catch him and his wife exchanging a forbidden look. But Touch the Sky knew better than to provoke him. Black Elk's jealous wrath was on the verge of exploding, and Honey Eater would bear the brunt of the blast.

Little Horse read these thoughts in his friend's troubled face. "Brother, everyone in the tribe knows that Honey Eater should have performed the squaw-taking ceremony with you, not Black Elk. Only when your enemies convinced her that you had deserted your tribe to return to the white man's world did she finally accept the gift of ponies from Black Elk. And then only because her father had crossed over to the Land of Ghosts, leaving her alone."

Both braves automatically made the cut-off sign, as one did when speaking of the dead.

"Now," Little Horse continued, "Black Elk hears the young girls in their sewing lodge, singing of the great and sad love between you and Honey Eater. The worm of jealousy cankers inside him. Once, though covered with hard bark, he was a fair man. But now he listens to his young cousin and no longer cares about his honor. The thought of the Arrows no longer holds him back."

Little Horse meant the sacred Medicine Arrows. These four ceremonial arrows symbolized the fate of the Cheyenne people. Bloodying a fellow Cheyenne also bloodied the Arrows— and thus the entire tribe. Usually, when violent emotions were brewing, the "thought of the Arrows" would hold a man back.

"Every word you have spoken," Touch the Sky said, "flies straight. And for Honey Eater's sake I must tread as cautiously as a wading bird. There was a time when Black Elk told me that Honey Eater would either accept his bride price or he and I must fight to the death."

"But she accepted it, buck."

Touch the Sky nodded. "She did. But his jealousy has grown into a beast with more heads than one man can chop off. Now I understand that it is not just Wolf Who Hunts Smiling who would feed me to the carrion birds. Despite his marriage, Black Elk and I must *still* fight to the death."

Buffalo Hiders

"Hold your horses, fellahs," Patch Orrick said. "I got something to show you."

Sid 'Long Rifle' Myers and Ace Ludlow sat their mounts on either side of Patch. Downwind below the three men, widely scattered in a huge draw just south of the Black Hills, a small herd of buffalo grazed the new grass.

"The hell, 'something to show you,'" Myers retorted. "You a goddamn schoolgirl with a four-leaf clover in your pocket? Look to our back trail, man! There's damn nigh 200 rifles eager to speak their piece."

Patch grinned, revealing a few brown stumps of remaining teeth. He wore filthy woollen chaps, stiff with old blood.

"Aw, that's mighty unspiritual of you, Sid. We've rode through some rough weather. Let them lubbers wait. You say ol' Ace here is a dumb sonofabitch? Well, I'm here to show you the buff is even dumber. Watch."

"Shee-*yit!*" Ace said, slapping his saddle. "Hail, yes, I'm dumb. That's a fack! Me and the buff!"

"Keep your voice down, you simple shit," Myers said.

Up close, Myers could see fleas leaping off both men's scalps. From one of the saddle scabbards on all three horses protruded the octagonal barrels of .53 Hawken rifles equipped with swivel-plate tripod mounts. The weapons accepted a half-ounce ball. To add insurance to this already superb buffalo-killing ball, most of the hunters fired a double charge: They increased the powder load from 100 to 200 grains of black powder. This diminished accuracy somewhat but greatly increased impact and distance.

From the other scabbard protruded the brass butt-plates of their "slaughter guns"—brand-new Volcanic lever-action repeaters. These could be loaded and 30 shots fired in less than a minute. The ammunition was waterproof, the weapon light. It did not always kill with one shot. But it required no cap or priming, no bullet mould or powder flask. It was ideal for rapid-fire killing at closer distances.

"Aw, c'mon, Sid," Patch said. "Le'me show you this here trick. It's slicker 'n' snot on a saddlehorn. Could come in handy, too."

"You telling me the straight?"

"Would a cow lick Lot's wife? *Course* I'm tellin' the straight."

Myers shrugged one shoulder in irritated surrender. By now he *was* mildly curious to see what Patch had on the spit. Ace Ludlow was indeed a soft-brain, a mean Missouri hardcase who had caught the dripping disease from a venereal-tainted Mandan—though it hadn't affected his deadly aim. But Patch, though nervous as a blue-blood horse and possessed of a mad, fire-and-brimstone glint to his eye, was crafty and useful.

"All right," he finally said. "Let's see this trick. But hurry it up, you're burning daylight."

He turned in the saddle and signalled for the group leaders to ride forward. Behind Myers and his two companions, spread out for nearly a half mile, was a virtual flotilla of men, animals, and equipment. Mule-drawn flatbed wagons were chockablock with provisions and weapons, kegs of black powder, tin cases of ball and primer caps, buffalo hides pressed flat into standard commercial "packs" of ten.

When the group leaders had ridden forward, Myers said, "Pass the word. I want every swinging peeder to form up into their hunt groups. But *nobody* cracks a cap until I give the word."

Myers didn't need to raise his voice to command authority. He was a huge, shaggy bear of a man, tall and looming and marked with menace even sitting slumped in his saddle. But beyond his physical appearance, every hunter in the group knew damn good and well who 'Long Rifle' Myers was—no one on the frontier had sold more buffalo robes to the greenhorns back East. And it was said he had killed at least 50 more for every one he had skinned, counting the entire herds they had run over blind cliffs called buffalo jumps. One U.S. Army general had proudly referred to him as "the worst enemy the red aboriginal ever had."

From his mountain man days, Myers carried a curved powder horn from a Rocky Mountain Sheep. Engraved in it were the boastful words:

I and the Gun
With our Brother Ball
In whatever fight
We equal all.

Judd Cole

His worship of the gun was handy: There was no question that public sentiment had recently shifted against the buffalo. So long as the buffalo ranged free, so too would the Red Peril. Not to mention that stampeding buffalo could ruin a track bed. And during shedding season, when they itched constantly, they knocked over telegraph poles while trying to scratch themselves.

"Well?" Myers demanded again of Patch. "You got a cob up your sitter? I'm waiting to see this consequential trick of yours."

"Wait here, boys."

Patch swung down from his mount and hobbled it. Then, since they were fairly close to the herd below, he selected his Volcanic repeater. Patch had earned his nickname because he was an incurable "blinker"—forced to wear an eyepatch when shooting because his non-aiming eye constantly winked open and distracted him. He slid the patch down now over his left eye. When it was in place, he was a deadly accurate shot.

Moving carefully, knowing it was smell he had to be careful of more than movement, Patch edged closer and took cover behind a hummock.

A moment later, Patch loosed a good imitation of a calf bawling in distress. Immediately, a cow came lumbering over to investigate. Patch rose for a moment and dropped her with one quick snap shot.

The rest of the herd continued to graze nearby as if nothing had happened. Patch repeated the bawl. Another cow trotted over. He shot her dead beside the first.

"Shee-*yit!*" Ace said. "Hail yes! *I* ain't that dumb!"

One after another, cows trotted over to their deaths each time Patch bawled like a calf. Soon dead buffalo littered the plains around him.

Myers' normally humorless face had creased in a wide, astounded grin. Behind him, the men were roaring with laughter. Several had fallen out of their saddles to roll on the ground, helpless with convulsive mirth.

"Hell 'n' furies!" one of them shouted. "Them buff is just like my woman. They keep fallin' for the same line of shit!"

"*Jee*-zus Katy Christ! *There* is your 'noble bison,' boys. Noble and stupid!"

"Just like the Innuns."

"They smell alike, too!"

Myers had enjoyed this little diversion. But the rest of the nearly deaf animals had finally been alerted to the presence of humans. Already the lead bulls were running toward the point positions and bellowing the stampede call. With buff hides currently fetching three dollars apiece back in the St. Louis settlements, Myers figured it was time to get to work.

"All right, boys!" he shouted to the group leaders behind him. "Remember, shoot for the gut, not the ribcage. A gutshot bleeds more. Now put at 'em!"

With a collective whoop, the long, curved line of hunters surged forward. Myers clucked at his horse, joining them. As was his habit, he hooked his left leg around the saddlehorn. Then he lay his rifle across it and took aim.

The air suddenly pulsed and vibrated with the static crackle of rapid, heavy, unrelenting gunfire. Sheets of lead enveloped the herd, blue feathers of smoke rose overhead, the acrid stink of cordite stained the air. Below, all was pandemonium: calves bawled, cows lowed, angry bulls bellowed. Now and then, through the swirling yellow dust raised by the herd, Myers spotted a tufted tail, a woolly hump, the chin whiskers of a bull.

But the fire was sustained and withering. Soon enough, the entire herd lay dead. The sweet stink of blood filled the air.

"That's the whole shootin' match!" Myers called out. "Hiders, get to it."

Using long, curved skinning knives, they stripped the hides from head to buttocks. Next the hides were scraped clean of fat and staked out in the sun to dry. Later, they would be pressed flat into packs for easy transporting.

While hider crews took care of this, other men went around cutting the tongues out. These delicacies were packed in barrels filled with brine for shipping back East.

"I want me a nice 'n' juicy hump steak," Patch said, inspecting one of the bloody corpses with his gleaming, Armageddon eyes. Some of them were already crawling with flies. "That ol' hump is so tender, you don't got to chew it."

"I want *me* a liver," Ace said. "That sumbitch so juicy, she quiver when you bite 'er. *Mmm,* them's good fixens, hail yes!"

Buffalo Hiders

But Myers wasn't listening. Instead, he was gazing at the carnage with a satisfied sheen in his eyes. Myers knew he would not truly rest easy until every "great shaggy" on the plains had been killed. And the first tribe he planned to kill off along with the buffalo was the Cheyenne.

Toward most tribes he was merely indifferent, as he was toward the world in general. But all that changed forever when Southern Cheyenne Dog Soldiers, a small band under the rebel Roman Nose, had attacked a settlement in Western Nebraska. Myers' wife and six-year-old boy were among the captives. In the long, suffering hours before they died, their eyelids had been sliced off and the prisoners staked out in the merciless sun. A sharp wooden stake had been pounded deep into his wife's sex; his son's genitals had been hacked off and crammed into the boy's mouth.

So now he had deliberately chosen to launch his war of buffalo extermination on the Cheyenne ranges. By bringing extinction to the bison, he also sounded the death knell of the red man. Profit *and* pleasure.

Newspapers all over the Missouri settlements had quoted his parting words when his keelboats sailed off: "I'll leave mountains of bone, rivers of blood, and it's damn hard work telling buffalo guts from Indian guts."

Chapter Two

Their sister the sun was burning straight overhead from a seamless blue sky when Black Elk raised his streamered lance to signal a halt beside a small rill.

Touch the Sky let his pony drink, then tethered her with rawhide in a lush patch of bunchgrass. Fresh meat was still scarce, so he notched a fire-hardened arrow in his bow and set off into the thickets in search of rabbits and other small game.

He threaded his way through a tangled deadfall, emerged quietly, then froze where he stood, on the edge of a small meadow bright with new flowers. His breath caught in his throat when he recognized the young woman.

Honey Eater.

She was alone, kneeling in the meadow. Touch

the Sky knew she must have slipped away, as was her custom, to gather white columbine petals. She would tuck them between wet leaves, keeping them fresh until she would braid them through her hair.

Still she hadn't spotted him. She wore a soft blue calico dress adorned with elk teeth, a fine bone choker. The sun reflected topaz on her flawless skin, revealed the slender and delicate bone structure of her limbs and finely sculpted cheeks.

He watched her carefully pluck another bunch of columbine petals and tuck them in the parfleche at her waist. His throat swelled tight with emotion, his pulse thudded loud in his ears.

As much as he wanted to call out her name, speak with her, he knew it was too risky. Black Elk or his spies could be anywhere. He was about to silently turn and leave. But just then, as if the wind had suddenly whispered her name, she glanced up and saw him.

The petals dropped from her fingers, unnoticed, to flutter away in the breeze.

She stood. The wind whipped her dress around her, molded it like a second skin to her slim legs and hips.

As if tugged by invisible ropes, he moved toward her, she toward him. In that moment all danger was forgotten, neither thought of anything but the other. She stepped up into his arms, and Touch the Sky pressed her animal-warm skin close to his. He buried his face in her hair, inhaling its fragrance.

"Have we both gone *wendigo*?" she said

finally, forcing herself to step back away from him. "Already Black Elk foams at the mouth if I even glance at you. What would he do if he saw us embracing?"

"What he would do to *me* is of no consequence. But for yourself, you do well to worry."

"I care not for myself! *I* would rather die and be done with this marriage to a man I have come to loathe with all my being. But if he or his enemies kill *you*, as they clearly plan to, then I swear by the sun and the earth I live on they will have to kill me, also."

Touch the Sky felt the sting of these words deep in his heart. "Have done with this talk of dying. Arrow Keeper spoke straight when he told me that life is but a short, warm moment. We will all soon enough feel the cold touch of death. You need not hurry things.

"As for me, here I stand, a living man. No brave in this tribe would lightly attempt to put me under."

"They *fear* you, yes, and rightly so. Your worst enemy admits you fight like ten men. But fear is not a good kind of respect. Black Elk, Wolf Who Hunts Smiling, and others in their Bull Whip soldier troop call you a *Mah-ish-ta-shi-da*. And since you helped the white miners build their railroad, Wolf Who Hunts Smiling now calls you White Man Runs Him."

Touch the Sky nodded. Cheyennes called whites *Mah-ish-ta-shi-da*, Yellow Eyes, because the first palefaces they ever saw were mountain men with jaundice.

Honey Eater said, "I, too, fear and hate most

whites. But some there are who try to speak one way to the Indian, a few are even trying to help us. But Wolf Who Hunts Smiling is like a dog in the hot moons, crazy and wild for blood and trouble. He claims he wants revenge on the soldiers who killed his father. But I think he has supped too full of hatred and meanness and false pride."

A crystal teardrop formed on Honey Eater's eyelash, then zigzagged down her cheek. "And that time when he lied, when he said you must swing from the pole by hooks or the buffalo hunt would be ruined. When the Council of Forty stripped him of his coup feathers as punishment, they also gave birth to a monster. All winter his hatred for you has festered. Touch the Sky, he is *for* you! I am afraid, be careful."

Touch the Sky was about to respond when a twig snapped behind them. He whirled, just in time to spot the distinctively cut feather of Black Elk's clan, visible above the tops of the bushes.

Fear for Honey Eater's safety iced his blood. If Black Elk found them together like this, Arrow Keeper's pleas would mean nothing—murder would sully the Arrows.

"Black Elk approaches!" he whispered. "Fly like the wind!"

But Honey Eater would have to cover the entire clearing to escape on the other side. And clearly there would not be enough time.

Abruptly, about a stone's throw away from the spot where Black Elk approached, Little Horse emerged. He was accompanied by the junior warrior whose unusual double braids had earned him the name Two Twists.

Even as Honey Eater overcame her panic and began to flee, Touch the Sky desperately pointed to Black Elk. Little Horse reacted now as he did on the field of battle: instinctively.

"Buck," he said loudly, pretending to be deep in an argument with Two Twists, "I will freely admit that Black Elk is a fine rider. Why, he rides as swift as the Archer shooting the nine suns! But *no* brave could have done this thing you speak of. I would bet a new blanket that I am right."

Hope rose like a tight bubble in his throat as Touch the Sky watched Black Elk's feather halt. He had risen to the bait! Even now, Honey Eater was escaping.

Little Horse dug an elbow into Two Twists's ribs. The younger Cheyenne hung fire only a moment before responding.

"Brother, I swear by the four directions he *did* this thing."

"Go find your mother's dug, little papoose, you are soft-brained for lack of milk! Not even a Comanche horseman could do this thing."

Now curiosity had Black Elk firmly by the tail. He was known as the tribe's most enthusiastic gambler. "*What* thing, bucks?" he demanded, crossing to join the other two and keen for a wager.

Relief surged through Touch the Sky as he watched Honey Eater make it safely to the cover of surrounding hawthorn thickets. He, too, slipped away from the clearing as Black Elk conferred with Little Horse and Two Twists, apparently setting a bet. It would be a cheap peace price indeed, Touch the Sky knew, if he only had to give his quick-thinking friend Little Horse a new blanket to cover a wager.

"But what does this thing mean?" Touch the Sky asked Arrow Keeper. "And who made it?"

The old shaman and his assistant stood before the slate-gray base of a cliff. It was covered with mysterious pictures painted in bright clay-based colors. Arrow Keeper had already deciphered the message in private council with Chief Gray Thunder.

He and Touch the Sky had lingered behind the rest of the column so Arrow Keeper could show his young shaman-apprentice the pictograph and demonstrate the art of interpretation. It had been painted on the cliff recently, beside a ford on the Weeping Woman River.

"It means trouble. And our Lakota cousins made it," Arrow Keeper said. "They knew we would pass this place, as we do each year at the beginning of the warm moons. Look at this."

The old man's face was as cracked and ridged as a peach pit. But the eyes swimming in all those wrinkles were keen and alert, still vital with the inner spirit of a warrior whose coup feathers trailed to the ground.

He pointed to a black feather drawn with charcoal. "What is this?"

"A feather. A crow feather?"

"*Ipewa,*" Arrow Keeper said. "Good. And what is this?"

"An elk with an arrow in it?"

"Yes. And this?"

"A buffalo."

"And what are these?"

"Boats?"

"And this?"

"The barrel is far too long, but clearly it is a rifle."

"*Ipewa.* This?"

"A . . . a soldier, but why are his eyes missing?"

The seams of Arrow Keeper's weather-rawed face deepened. "This means that the blue-bloused soldiers have deliberately decided not to see."

"Not to see what, father?"

"Be patient, buck, soon enough you will take the meaning. Now, have ears for my words. The black feather means the message is to the entire Cheyenne people, symbolized by the crow feathers our braves wear in their war bonnets. We know who made it by the elk shot through with an arrow, the sign of a Sioux band known as the Elk Eaters. This band lives far to the east of the main Sioux homeland, on the huge reservation the Yellow Eyes call the Indian Territory.

"Their chief, Starving Bull, was one of the first Indian leaders to make medicine with whites. He believed their lies and signed the talking papers called treaties. Now he knows those words, like most words uttered by palefaces, were bent. And he has sent messengers with this warning."

For a long moment Arrow Keeper paused, turning to stare toward the direction of the sacred Black Hills and the center of the

Cheyenne world. Whatever he saw in that distant gaze made his eyes cloud over with worry.

"The three boats," he continued, "are white men's keelboats. The rifle with such a long barrel tells us they are hunters with the finest weapons, capable of killing at incredible distances. A party of hunters is coming in vast numbers to destroy our buffalo herds. And they have the blessing of the blue-bloused soldiers, who know that once Uncle Pte the buffalo is dead and gone, the red man will not be far behind."

Arrow Keeper looked at Touch the Sky. The old shaman's frown deepened the furrow between his eyebrows.

"Little brother, this is no mere song of sadness for the red man's plight. Starving Bull would not have sent messengers this far unless strong bad medicine is on its way even now to meet us.

"Place these words in your sash. The buffalo is as important to the red man as gold is to the white man. And what does the white man do when his precious gold is threatened? Already, I fear, the slaughter has begun. So make ready your battle rig, for soon Gray Thunder's Cheyenne will be locked in a bloody war."

Soon Gray Thunder's tribe had resettled in their summer camp at the fork of the Powder and the Little Powder. A council was immediately called to discuss the ominous warning left by the Sioux.

"Cousin, the sign is good for us," Wolf Who Hunts Smiling said soon after the council was over. "But it is bad for White Man Runs Him. He gloated when he was selected to lead warriors against these hair-faced hunters. But finally, the 'visionary' has encountered a beast that make-believe magic and two-tongued treachery will not slay."

Wolf Who Hunts Smiling, his older cousin Black Elk, and Swift Canoe were all seated around the meat racks behind Black Elk's tipi. It was customary to meet here when members of the Bull Whip soldier society had secret schemes brewing. Their sister the sun had gone to her resting place. Now fires leaped and danced throughout the camp.

"This warning from the Sioux," Wolf Who Hunts Smiling continued, "about white hunters destroying Uncle Pte. It could not have arrived at a better time. You heard River of Winds make his scouting report to the Councillors this morning. Indeed, it touched on you directly."

Black Elk nodded. River of Winds was one of the tribe's most reliable scouts. Recently, forced to travel far south in search of the buffalo herds, the tribe had narrowly escaped destruction at the hands of Kiowas and Comanches. Now River of Winds had returned from a long scout of their enemies' homeland, bearing ominous news: There were reliable signs that a large group of warriors, led by the fierce Comanche named Big Tree, was preparing to ride north—perhaps to mount a revenge strike for recent Cheyenne victories.

"The Councillors spoke one way on this thing," Wolf Who Hunts Smiling added. "Until we know the Kiowa-Comanche plans, you, as our battle chief, must keep a large war party near camp at all times. At no point will Touch the Sky have more than 20 braves in his group. And as you saw, he rode out with a few good braves but hardly the pick of the best warriors."

"Nor can our Sioux cousins help him," said Swift Canoe. "Stands Looking Back has taken his band north, past the Marias River, hunting ponies. Even if those Sioux scouts who painted the warning go after them, it will be many sleeps before they find them."

Black Elk continued to scowl darkly, unconvinced by any of this talk about the downfall of Touch the Sky. He wore a bone breastplate which gleamed dully in the light from the nearest clan fire. He was heavily muscled for an Indian, and made even fiercer looking by the dead, leathery flap of his left ear—it had been severed in battle by a Bluecoat saber. Black Elk had calmly picked up his ear, then killed the soldier; after the battle, he sewed his own ear back on with buckskin thread.

Now he said, "You and Swift Canoe have celebrated his death before. Yet, his stink is still with us. Why should *this* time be any different?"

Wolf Who Hunts Smiling flashed his wily grin. The swift-as-minnow eyes darted back and forth between the other two.

"Because, cousin," he replied, "it will be a double-pronged attack. While his enemies outside the tribe lay their bead sights on him, his many enemies *within* the tribe will be acquiring fresh ammunition to use against him. I care not which flank he is killed from, just that he is killed."

Black Elk still scowled. But his hotheaded cousin was an effective speaker, and by now Black Elk's curiosity was piqued.

"Hear me, buck," he said impatiently. "Break the shell and dig down to the meat. What is your plan?"

"Plenty of meat, cousin, if you would only take a moment to chew on it. Recall, it has not been many moons since White Man Runs Him helped the white miners build their path for the iron horse."

"True enough, but why speak of that? The peace price they paid was generous. The blankets and food helped the tribe survive the cold moons."

"Indian braves east of the Great Waters eat paleface rations, too, but do *you* call them warriors? Many feel that the 'peace price' was too dear, that we sold part of our freedom. They also saw that this white man, Caleb Riley, already knew Touch the Sky. This alarms many and suggests that he is drinking from the same pond with the Yellow Eyes. Now it is time to fuel those flames higher again."

"This Touch the Sky," Swift Canoe put in, "he carries the white man's stink on him for life. But clearly, Arrow Keeper and certain other hoary-headed elders dote on him and believe his tales of 'visions.' Hiding behind such false paint, he hopes to take over the tribe. He would even put on the old moccasin with our women."

No names were mentioned. But Black Elk's face stiffened at the hard truth of these last words. "Putting on the old moccasin" was the Cheyenne way of referring to an unmarried buck who wanted to rut with a married woman. Everyone present knew that, in this case, the "old moccasin" was Black Elk's wife, Honey Eater.

"What we must do is as clear as blood on new snow," Wolf Who Hunts Smiling said. "We must be careful, subtle as the change from dawn to full day. But we must paint a picture through suggestions and rumors. A picture which suggests Touch the Sky's treachery without saying his name. A picture which hints that those same white miners are back now to profit from the destruction of our herds. A picture which shows how Touch the Sky *pretends* to fight them while secretly spying for them."

Black Elk shook his head, looking at Wolf Who Hunts Smiling. "Cousin, are you a dog returning to its vomit? Think, buck. How did you lose your coup feathers? By starting lies about Touch the Sky. Are you looking for your own grave by doing so again?"

"This time, cousin, not at all. This Touch the Sky, I know his tricks. He puts the trance glaze over his eyes and quickens his breathing. Thus he gives the doting old fools gooseflesh. It is easy sport.

"So we *must* do as I suggest," Wolf Who Hunts Smiling insisted. "Else, how can we fight the 'visions' of White Man Runs Him?

Pick my words up and place them in your sash, cousin. We have circled our quarry long enough. I, for one, have plans. Plans *he* will never abide. It is long past time to close for the kill."

Chapter Three

For three sleeps Touch the Sky led his war party due east, toward the sacred Black Hills. It was in these vast ranges that the smaller herds joined forces for the great migratory stampedes which carried them west. And it was near here where the white hunters would first disembark from their keelboats to begin the bloody slaughter of Uncle Pte.

The division of Gray Thunder's warriors had reflected tribal tensions and a divided council: Black Elk, Wolf Who Hunts Smiling, and their fellow Bull Whips had all remained in camp to defend against a possibly imminent Kiowa-Comanche attack. Touch the Sky and Little Horse, along with Tangle Hair and many of his fellow Bowstring troopers, were to take the fight to the white hiders. One thing the Headmen did agree on: These paleface death merchants could not go unchallenged.

Arrow Keeper and Touch the Sky had conducted the Renewal of the Arrows ceremony for all the warriors. Now each brave wore his single-horned crow-feather war bonnet. Each also carried his own personal medicine or totem with him for special courage in battle. They had all fashioned strong new bows of green oak and strung them with thin but tough buffalo sinew. Ammunition was scarce, some braves possessing fewer than ten rounds. Their firearms ranged from small-caliber but sturdy British trade rifles to Little Horse's deadly scattergun with its four revolving barrels.

On their third day out, Little Horse nudged his buckskin pony up beside Touch the Sky.

"Brother, you have sent out no flankers or point riders. Should I scout ahead now? We will soon cross the first stampede trails. Our enemy may be anywhere."

"No need," Touch the Sky said. "Cast your eye around you, buck. As far as a man could ride in one full sleep, there is no cover. The Yellow Eyes are many more than we are, they are heavy with equipment. We will spot them first. Besides, we need only watch for the buffalo birds to know the herds must be near."

Little Horse nodded, his face drawn tight with worry. And the sturdy little warrior did indeed cast his eye about him: the vast, slate-gray dome of an overcast sky fit like a tight lid over the brown expanse of the plains. Here and there a scrub oak or a stunted, wind-twisted cottonwood broke up the otherwise monotonous landscape.

"As you say," Little Horse said, "there is no cover, and if our Sioux cousins spoke straight, our enemies are many more than we are. Let us pray we *do* spot them first."

Touch the Sky glanced at his friend. "Is today a good day to die?" he demanded.

For a moment a grin replaced Little Horse's mask of worry. "Not for a fighting Cheyenne!" he replied.

It was an old rallying cry between them. Little Horse turned around and loosed the tribe's shrill war cry: *"Hi-ya, hii-ya!"* As one, the warriors raised their streamered lances and repeated it.

Hearing the warriors shout behind them, Touch the Sky's pony trembled with the urge to break stride and run hard. But the tall youth pulled back on her hair bridle, holding her in and conserving her strength for the trials ahead.

The high-spirited blood mare was one of the favorites in his string. He had singled her out during a recent pony hunt, cutting her from a herd of mustangs grazing the foothills of the Bighorn Mountains. He had broken her in the way an Indian always breaks a good pony: not like the whites, with blindfolds and water-starving and beatings designed to break the horse's spirit.

Instead, he simply leaped on the horse's back and held on for dear life. He rode her hard for the better part of a morning, until she faltered and blew foam. From that time on he had become her master, the pony an extension of his own strong body, of his own indomitable will to win.

Now the brave named Tangle Hair rode up beside them. He was one of the first Bowstring troopers to openly declare his loyalty to Touch the Sky. This was after watching the tall warrior count first coup against land-grabber Wes Munro's white militia in the famous Tongue River Battle, the bloody struggle to save the Cheyenne homeland.

"Brothers," he greeted his friends, "a thing has been worrying me. It is a deadly enough enemy we ride out to face. But while we beat the bushes, it is the snakes hidden in our sleeping robes that may kill us."

Both of his comrades took the meaning of this: Nearly everyone riding with Touch the Sky knew that Wolf Who Hunts Smiling and Black Elk had lately been meeting fellow conspirators behind Black Elk's tipi. All this new activity had started after Arrow Keeper had deciphered the fatal pictograph left by the Sioux.

"Clearly," Little Horse said, "Touch the Sky's enemies hope to link him once again with the *Mah-ish-ta-schi-da*. The tribe does not hate the white miners enough. But they surely hate these hunters."

"Black Elk and his cousin," Tangle Hair said, "have not listened closely to Arrow Keeper and the other elders who were once great war leaders. They have the killing skills, true. No one kills better. But there is more to the Warrior Way than mere skill with weapons."

These words flew straight-arrow, and Touch the Sky nodded with the others. Two things were admired in a warrior society: bravery and generosity, including compassion when it was due. Wolf Who Hunts Smiling and Black Elk had plenty of the former, very little of the latter. As a result, they were feared but not truly respected. Worse, they were also dangerous.

"All these things you say are straight enough," Touch the Sky said. "The time is coming when my lance will tip against theirs, and the Arrows will be sullied when a Cheyenne sheds tribal blood. But for now our enemy is more clearly marked. We had best watch for them. Out here, bucks, he who is first spotted is also the first sent under."

The first sign of serious trouble was the vast flock of carrion birds. Sister Sun was creeping down toward her resting place, but still it was easy to see that thousands of scavengers darkened the sky, circling, diving, fighting for the best positions below.

The Cheyennes had fallen silent as they climbed the last, long rise which separated them from sight of the ground beneath the birds. A vagrant breeze shifted slightly, and the stench hit them broadside. Several of them gagged at the putrid, decaying stink.

Touch the Sky heard coyotes and wolves snapping and growling below. The tantalized animals resentfully slunk off as the first Cheyennes topped the rise and stared at the sight below in the draw.

"Uncle Pte," somebody said out loud, and the words hung long in the loathsome air like an accusation.

Judd Cole

Touch the Sky's emotions ranged from unbelieving shock through seething rage to gut-
wrenching sorrow at sight of the deliberate
carnage. Dead buffalo lay everywhere, so thick
with flies the air hummed like the white man's
talking wires.

The waste was incredible, and each Cheyenne
felt as if he were seeing something sinful, something too awful and unholy to talk about. There
lay the rotting meat, the hooves and horns that
could have made cups and utensils, the sinews
that could have made thread and strong bow
strings, the hair that should have been woven
into ropes, the bladders that should have become
water bags.

They rode slowly through the field of slaughter, scattering the parasites. A wagon with a
badly broken axle had been left behind. As the
sun flamed into her last, bloodred blaze of glory,
Touch the Sky ordered the wagon broken up and
a huge fire built of the wood. The smoke and
light kept scavengers and flies off. But the fire
also glistened with grisly beauty on the raw, red
humps dotting the plains all around them.

"Brothers!" Touch the Sky said after his braves
had tethered their mounts and eaten a meager
meal of dried venison and bitterroot. "Uncle Pte
has been desecrated in numbers too great to
fathom. This thing cannot stand. We cannot
just ride away as if strong bad medicine has
not contaminated us. The stink of a bad death
is on *us* too! Only a blood-cleansing ceremony
might give us our good medicine back."

No one questioned this important spiritual

decision. Touch the Sky's reputation as a powerful shaman became the stuff of permanent Cheyenne lore after he and Little Horse had ridden north to the Bear Paw Mountains. There, Touch the Sky saved the Cheyenne band of Chief Shoots Left Handed by invoking the rarely granted Iron Shirt magic. Seth Carlson and his mountain regiment had gaped in unbelieving shock as their bullets, fired point blank, had failed to score a single kill.

Now the warriors knew what must be done. The custom was clear concerning the remains of buffalo killed without the authorization of formal Hunt Law. That night, while the orange-tipped flames burned down to a heap of glowing embers, the braves moved methodically through the killing field.

With tomahawks, hatchets, and battle axes they hacked each head free of its body. The skulls were lined up neatly in row after row, the dead eyes facing east to catch the first sight of the rising sun.

That night, while the braves stood in grim silence, Touch the Sky chanted a long renewal prayer to the Great Medicine Man. While he chanted, his voice a lulling sing-song, a lone coyote howled from the surrounding darkness. It began with a shrill bark, followed by a series of sharp yelps ending in a long, trembling howl.

"My heart is a stone toward the hair faces who did this," he announced when the chant was over. "There is no soft place left in me. So long as they walk the same earth I live on, there will be no peace in my heart. Now, sleep. We will post sentries, and all must rise before the sun. You know what must be done. Uncle Pte cries out to the heavens for revenge."

Next morning, as the sun sent her first weak beams out to burn off the morning mist, each Cheyenne stood over a rotting buffalo corpse.

As one, they raised their left arms out over the corpse, following Touch the Sky's example. When he slashed his own arm deep with his knife, they unhesitatingly copied his example.

Even as their warm blood dripped onto the tacky, rotting corpses, Touch the Sky called out:

"Our blood for buffalo blood! The fate of Uncle Pte is the fate of the red man. Brothers, it will be a child's game to follow the paleface sign. Let us ride now. I say again, this desecration on our ancient hunting grounds will *not* stand! From this time forth, we must send our thoughts toward revenge and nothing else!"

He thrust his streamered lance high as a mighty war cry rose into the air. Touch the Sky grabbed a handful of mane and swung up onto his pony. The rest followed suit. But even before the last Cheyenne had left the draw, the carrion birds were circling again.

Clearly, the buffalo hiders had no fear of being followed.

Their horses and heavily laden wagons tore up the plains almost as thoroughly as a herd of stampeding buffalo. But they had no need for caution. Out here they moved like Lord Grizzly in the forest, commanding all they saw.

These were not hearty white pioneers or green military recruits. They were well-armed, expert marksmen and experienced plainsmen.

Touch the Sky hoped to turn that confidence of victory against them. Just how, he wasn't sure yet. During his warrior training under Black Elk, the older brave had emphasized that the element of surprise was vital against a vastly superior force.

But how, he agonized yet again, would he maintain secrecy of movement out here where waist-high buffalo grass was often the only cover so far as the eye could see? How mount a nighttime assault with 20 warriors against a virtual stockade? He did not yet know the exact numbers of the paleface hiders. But the plowed-up swath of ground hinted at hundreds.

One sleep after the Cheyenne started trailing the hair faces, they made contact with their enemy.

It was Tangle Hair who first sounded the warning. The band had halted at an underground-fed pool to water their mounts. Tangle Hair walked out ahead of the others and knelt, placing the fingertips of his right hand lightly on the ground. He stayed that way a long time.

"I feel riders approaching," he finally announced to the others. "Not many, but they are close enough to watch for."

Sure enough, they soon spotted a group of three riders, still specks on the horizon.

"Do we flee?" Little Horse said.

Touch the Sky shook his head. "For what good reason? Our presence here will soon be known to the whites, if it is not already. These riders will either stop when they see us, or they will ride on with a message for us. If they have some treachery in mind, may their white god have mercy on their souls. How do you counsel?"

"You speak words I can pick up and pocket," Little Horse said. "Let us wait and see which way the wind sets."

"They appear to have stopped," a Bowstring trooper named Bear Tooth reported. "No doubt they have spotted us."

The Cheyenne, curious, lined up to watch the horizon. They were still well out of rifle range, so no one worried about covering down.

"What are they doing?" someone said.

Tangle Hair, squinting, one hand over his eyes, finally said, "I believe one of them is lying upon the ground. Perhaps he is injured?"

"Hair faces are a queer lot," Bear Tooth said. "Perhaps this one sleeps best under a blazing sun."

"Or perhaps these white men have gone Wendigo from the open spaces," Tangle Hair said. "The plains have driven more than one paleface mad."

But Touch the Sky suddenly frowned. His 'shaman eye' saw something suspicious in this.

"Brothers," he said, "this is trouble, count upon it. We must—"

At that moment there was a sound like a water bag bursting. One of the ponies drinking from the pond, a sturdy buckskin, abruptly dropped to its front knees as an arc of blood spumed from its flank. A heartbeat later it lay on its side, heaving in death agonies.

The Cheyenne, shocked to the very core of their souls, were too stupefied at first with disbelief to react. No bullet could possibly fly this far, shot by a marksman they could barely see! But the next moment a big chunk flew from Little Horse's rawhide shield, and Touch the Sky shouted the order to retreat.

Chapter Four

His war party secure in a large river thicket, Touch the Sky called a council of all his braves. It was not the Cheyenne way for a leader to dictate, but to determine the collective will of the group.

"The *Mah-ish-ta-schi-da* have always come armed with weapons superior to ours," Little Horse said bitterly. "When we had only bows, they had muskets. When the English Grandmother's soldiers gave us muskets, the Yellow Eyes had percussion weapons. Now we finally have percussion rifles, and *they* have medicine-blessed firesticks, bullets blessed with eyes so they travel farther than a red man can see."

"My best pony is dead," said a brave named Ute Killer. "But hard though the loss, I do not think my pony was the target."

"No," Touch the Sky agreed. "These brave white slaughterers of the defenseless buffalo would not trouble with warning shots. One of *us* was surely the target. But the ball which dropped Ute Killer's pony must be the huge buffalo ball we have heard of. This means they have powerful rifles strong enough to handle a double charge of black powder."

"And such a charge," Tangle Hair said, "is indeed powerful. But like a spring-drunk mustang, it wanders more, too."

"It did not wander far enough," Ute Killer said bitterly.

"It is hard," Touch the Sky said, "but we must accept this bitter truth. We are in some of the most barren land on our ranges. We are up against hundreds of rifles which reach twice the range of our few best. If *we* were choosing our course, we could ensure some cover by sticking to these river thickets, by seeking out rocky spines. But our enemy follows Uncle Pte, and we must follow our enemy no matter what the trials and hardships."

"Then what is left to us?" Bear Tooth said. "Will you turn us all into ghost warriors so that bullets cannot find us?"

Bear Tooth's mild scorn reflected the fear and frustration of this mission. Little Horse started to defend his friend, but Touch the Sky laid a hand on his shoulder to quiet him.

"No, brother," Touch the Sky said patiently to Bear Tooth. "There is a time and a place for everything. The spirit path is not to be the way this time."

"Then what is?"

Touch the Sky knew that his vastly outnumbered warriors were on the verge of losing heart in this seemingly hopeless battle. It was critical to take the bull by the horns now, or his mission was in serious danger of failure. And failure, in this case, might well mean the extinction of the Cheyenne people—indeed, of the entire Red Nation.

"We cannot hide. Neither can we sit still and become targets. Therefore we depend on two things. Our superior ponies, and a war to unstring our enemy's nerves."

There was a long silence while these words were considered. Then several of the others murmured agreement.

"We cannot let the grass grow under us," Touch the Sky added. "I need two braves with good ponies to volunteer with me. I ask only for bucks who do not fear the sting of death, for it will be a fool's mission if ever one was planned."

There was no time for anyone else to debate: Little Horse and Tangle Hair immediately spoke up.

"There are no fools in my clan, brother. But I am keen for sport," Little Horse said. "I have no plans to die in my tipi."

"And I am curious to test my new pony," Tangle Hair said. "This will put her up against it."

"It will," Touch the Sky said. "Count upon it."

The council over, Touch the Sky, Little Horse, and Tangle Hair tended to their battle rigs.

Touch the Sky made sure he had a primer
cap behind the loading gate of his Sharps, a
round in the chamber. He was well supplied with
black powder, but critically short on bullets.
Fortunately, his foxskin quiver was stuffed full
of new, fire-hardened arrows.

He was battle-tested enough by now to know
that weapons alone did not win a fight. Fighting
spirit was important, as was the possession of
strong medicine. He and Arrow Keeper had
already conducted the Renewal of the Medicine
Arrows. Now it was up to Maiyun, the Good
Supernatural.

Again, as he honed the single sharp edge of
his obsidian knife on a whetstone, Touch the
Sky's mind wandered to the great vision he had
experienced at sacred Medicine Lake—the same
vision Arrow Keeper had experienced first. That
vision foretold greatness for Touch the Sky,
who would become the greatest war chief in
Cheyenne history.

But the vision also foretold great suffering
first. And Arrow Keeper's words returned to
haunt him now: *A medicine vision can be either
a revelation or a curse. An enemy's bad medicine
may place a false vision over our eyes, and we may
act upon it, aiding our enemies and destroying
those whom we seek to help.*

"Brother?"

Slowly, as if surfacing from the bottom of a
deep pool, Touch the Sky's thoughts returned
to the present. Little Horse, busy tightening the
stone tip on his lance with rawhide thongs, was
staring at him. So was Tangle Hair. His next

remark showed that he had read something of his friend's thoughts.

"Brother, I have seen the mark of the warrior buried in your hair. The hand of the Great Medicine Man is in this thing. Whatever fight lies ahead, take heart. If we must die, it will be the glorious death of warriors."

Touch the Sky only nodded, knowing his friend was trying to hearten all three of them. But the tall youth knew it would be a thin, pale sort of glory indeed if paleface hiders were permitted to exterminate Uncle Pte.

"Prepare to ride," he told his band.

Picking up the hiders' trail had been child's play. Now, far out on the unbroken plain, they could see the dark outline of their enemy's camp.

"Halt here," Touch the Sky said. "By now the palefaces know we are out here. We dare not ride closer at this pace or their long guns will drop us."

Touch the Sky knew that these whites would also have picket outposts where guards stood watch. He gathered his braves around him.

"I have always talked one way to you. I will do so now. That long shot which sent Ute Killer's pony under, it was a reminder for us. A reminder that the time for mourning Uncle Pte is over. Now it is time for *this*."

Touch the Sky brandished a piece of charcoal. "This day we paint for death. And the paint remains until our enemy is vanquished or the rain washes it from our dead skulls."

His mouth a grim, determined slit, Touch the Sky lined his warriors up. Then he decorated each man's face with black charcoal—the symbol of joy at the death of an enemy.

"Now," he said to Little Horse and Tangle Hair when he had finished, "you know the plan. Let us strike while enough light remains."

Their ponies were rested now, had grazed and drunk their fill. As planned, the three braves rode out in single file, presenting minimal targets for their enemy. They were not attempting to hide— just the opposite. Each man held his lance high, blood-red streamers fluttering in the wind.

They wanted to be seen. This was a mission of defiance, not destruction. Touch the Sky had decided on the one action which would surely put his Cheyenne warriors in fighting fettle: three braves were going to count first coup on an entire buffalo camp.

When the dark outlines of the circular camp began to show distinct forms and shapes, Touch the Sky also spotted a tall wooden mast rising from a buckboard. From it, an American flag snapped in the wind. The Cheyenne dropped his lance, the signal to begin evasive riding tactics.

His high-spirited mare needed little encouragement from him. The moment Touch the Sky leaned low over her neck and loosed a war cry, the tough little blood laid her ears back and surged beneath him. All three riders swung from the left to the right, hiding behind first one flank, then the other, discouraging sharpshooters. Their well-trained horses, meantime, rode in anything but a straight line.

As he flashed over his pony's back, changing sides frequently, always clinging low on the pony's neck, Touch the Sky watched the white man's fortification draw closer. He could see the first marksmen, crouched behind tripod-mounted rifles; he saw sturdy breastworks made from new pine logs; he saw men running about like agitated insects, pointing in amazement toward this trio of suicidal Indians attacking them. Buckboards, crates, hide-presses and other equipment formed a defensive perimeter around the camp.

Rifles spat black curls of smoke. Now and then a half-ounce buffalo ball hurtled past his ears with a whirring vengeance. Once the tough little pony stumbled, just as Touch the Sky was changing flanks. As she tilted hard to the left, he swung his weight hard to the right, adding his strength to hers. The mare balanced on the feather edge of tumbling hard, then recovered and flew ahead again.

"Hi-ya!" Little Horse yipped to rally the Cheyennes and the ponies. "Hii-*ya!*"

Now they could hear the solid roar of big, double-charged Hawkens, the lighter, more rapid cracking of the Volcanic lever-action repeaters. Divots of grass flew into their faces, plumes of yellow dust rose as bullets scarred the earth all around them. The air was so thick with lead that Touch the Sky almost thought a swarm of bees was attacking.

Already a bullet had creased her glossy flank, but the mare only surged forward even harder, keen for the charge. Despite the metallic fear coating his tongue, Touch the Sky felt her wild blood humming with the power of unbridled speed and motion. As he merged his will and destiny with his pony's, he drew added strength from her animal instincts, she from his human courage.

A sharp tug at his left legging told him a bullet had nearly found him. But now the three braves were almost on the camp. He felt the mare go airborne, saw a flatbed wagon flash by just below.

Touch the Sky heaved himself up onto his pony's back again. Everywhere, shocked and frightened and enraged palefaces parted before him like water before a prow. Rifles spat fire, so many his ears stung. But Touch the Sky bore inexorably toward the buckboard and the American flag.

His course took him past a trio of whites who were too busy gawking at him in disbelief to draw a tight bead on him. One was a huge bear of a man, his face stamped with the menacing authority of a leader; another had crazy-bright eyes and wore filthy woollen chaps crusted with old blood; the third grinned the lopsided, foolish grin of a man gone crazy-by-thunder. For a moment Touch the Sky's eyes found those of the man he guessed was the leader, and those eyes sent him a promise—the promise of a sure and hard death.

But now Tangle Hair whooped loudly and veered left, scattering a group of remounts. They panicked, broke through their rope corral, and scattered out onto the plains. Little Horse, at a hard gallop, hooked his lance under the guy rope of a huge U. S. Army tent. It collapsed in a wild tangle, snaring the men who had leaped inside for cover. They panicked and began punching and kicking one another in their desperation to get free.

Even as the tent collapsed, Touch the Sky gripped the flagpole and yanked it free of its bracket mount. Holding it cocked under one arm like a lance, he cleared the camp and leaped over a wagon on the far side. A moment later Tangle Hair and Little Horse joined him. A hail of lead and curses chased them out onto the open plains.

Still in clear sight, Touch the Sky whirled his pony and let her dance while he faced the enemy.

"We have counted first coup, buffalo killers!" he shouted in English. "For mere sport you have come to destroy our way of life. Now Cheyenne braves are here to tell you, we will destroy *you!* Remember, as you watch your brothers die a hard death one by one, the red man did not send out the first soldier. We only sent out the second."

Despite his hatred for these murdering butchers, Touch the Sky refused to desecrate the flag of their nation—the same nation which had taught him its language and history but denied him the promise of his rights as a man. True, white man's culture had produced these filthy, flea-ridden, Indian-hating slaughterers of the buffalo. But it had also produced his white parents, who loved him strong and true; Corey

Robinson, his childhood friend who risked his life to save the Cheyenne people from a Pawnee attack; Tom and Caleb Riley, simple frontiersmen who treated men according to their merit, not their skin color.

There were indeed decent palefaces, and this flag symbolized their decency. So now, while bullets nipped at his ears, he defiantly rammed the flagpole securely into the dirt of the plains.

"May the white god pity you!" he shouted. "For the red god will not!"

Then it was time to ride hard toward the horizon, as the first outraged hiders raced for their mounts to give chase.

Chapter Five

Counting first coup on the white hiders accomplished little of practical value. But it was a great moral victory for Touch the Sky and his vastly outnumbered band.

Those remaining behind had watched their Cheyenne comrades disappear into an inferno of black smoke and screaming lead. Surely, many of them told each other with their eyes, this Touch the Sky has finally found his own grave—nothing living could have survived this death trap! Small wonder, Touch the Sky told himself, that a few of them had turned pale, as if seeing ghosts, when the trio rode back.

In a gesture of boastful defiance, Little Horse and Tangle Hair had stolen trophies: Tangle Hair wore a slouch beaver hat he seized while sailing past a scurrying paleface. Little Horse managed to wrestle an Army saber from the hands of a drunken camp defender.

As previously arranged, the Cheyennes quickly set out, heading due west from their present camp. They rode hard until nightfall. Then, when their tired ponies began to blow foam, they made a false camp—embers left glowing and dirt piled to look like sleeping bodies. A few ponies were left to graze on long tethers. The Cheyennes then moved well past the decoy and made a cold camp for themselves. If hiders followed their trail, the noise from attacking the decoy site would alert the real camp.

"Brothers," Touch the Sky said as soon as the second camp was ready, "there is no time to let today's victory turn cold. Nor is it enough to merely surprise our enemy. I told you we must count on two things, our superior ponies and a war of nerves. Our ponies have performed well this day. Now, while Uncle Moon owns the sky, we must launch our war of nerves."

He glanced around at the circle of solemn faces, lighted only by moonwash. In this light, the streaks of black charcoal were a stark contrast to their skin.

"A few of us will return to their camp this very night. You all know it is not the Cheyenne way to mount a mission after dark. But brothers, count on it, this time the Cheyenne tribe is up against it. We are fighting now for the survival of the buffalo, and thus, of our people.

"Little Horse and I are both experienced in nighttime movement. He will ride with me. We need two more braves. They must not be men who hope to die in their sleep."

The fighting spirit was strong again thanks to the day's great victory. Five braves volunteered. Touch the Sky selected two Bowstring troopers—Dull Knife and the brave who had expressed frustration earlier, Bear Tooth. Touch the Sky had seen both men fight like angry wolverines at the Tongue River Battle against land-grabber Wes Munro and his hair-face militiamen. Both were also loyal to the Bowstring leader, Spotted Tail, one of Touch the Sky's few influential allies in the tribe.

The Bowstrings followed the example of Little Horse and Touch the Sky: All four warriors prepared by wrapping their heads in skins and blankets. They remained in total darkness until their pupils were as huge as melon seeds. Now, when Touch the Sky unwrapped his head, the solid darkness was reduced to a mist which revealed distances and outlines not visible before.

"We will not ride in close," he said to the others. "Not in such flat country without cover. But they will have outlying sentries. So tie these around your ponies' hooves."

He handed each buck pieces of thick rawhide to mute the sound of the horses.

"Dull Knife?"

"I hear you, Touch the Sky."

"Your pony has white markings?"

"She has."

"For tonight, trade her for a darker one. No bone chokers, no elk-tooth necklaces, *nothing* which might rattle or reflect light."

The rest nodded, Bear Tooth removing the heavy necklace for which he was named.

"Check your battle rigs," Touch the Sky said. "Have everything to hand so you can grab it in total darkness. Then rig your ponies. Before we mount, each man must rub his exposed skin well with mud. Uncle Moon is bright tonight. The same light that shows on an enemy glows on a friend."

Tangle Hair, chaffing at being left behind this time, was placed in charge of the remaining warriors. Then the four Cheyennes rode out in single file. Touch the Sky made sure the moon did not backlight them as they retraced their steps toward the hiders' camp.

"I damn near shit strawberries when that buck spoke up in good English," Sid Myers said. "Hell, I still don't credit my own ears. *That* red son of the plains has got himself a white man's education some place."

"An Innun what palavers English dies the same as the rest," Patch Orrick said. "A *bullet* don't care if you kin quote Shakespeare."

Patch's woolly chaps looked filthy and crusted even in the flickering firelight. The patch he wore to cover his "nervous eye" when shooting was now pushed up high on his forehead.

"That tent fixed?" Myers demanded.

Patch nodded. "All they done was bust a guy-line and shake up a few of the boys. Hell, it was all talk and no walk. They done less damage than a fart in a twister. You ask me, they're just tryin' to four-flush us."

"Maybe. But the Cheyenne ain't known for bluffing. They sure's hell wasn't four-flushing when they sent my family under."

"What the hell set 'em off this time?"

"Had to be they found dead buff. Now they're on the warpath. This today was just a taste of the fixens they got on the spit for us."

Patch laughed. His eyes had a mad-preacher sheen to them in the eerie orange light. "Let it come! We got the firepower of a by-God Army division."

Myers nodded, though he looked less sanguine than his companion. He had just maneuvered a buckboard into place, closing the defensive perimeter around their huge camp. Myers tied the reins to the brake and swung down, whistling to catch the attention of Ace Ludlow.

"Ace! You got a cob up your sitter? Unhitch this team and turn the mules out to graze."

"Shee-*yit!* Me 'n' the mother-ruttin' mules, dumb sonsabitches! *Hail* yes, that's a fack!"

"I swan, that crazy bastard gives me belly flies," Patch said. "Why do you keep his simple ass around?"

"He shoots plumb, don't he? He don't have your steady hand, but he can drop buff better 'n any three of the rest. That's all that matters to me."

Myers tied his holster to his thigh. Then he slid the Colt Navy revolver out and rolled the cylinder, checking his loads.

The leader of the hiders stared out into the vast, grainy darkness beyond the perimeter. His eyes slitted as some vague warning moved up his spine like a scurrying centipede. He was forced to raise his voice above the clamor in camp. Whiskey and rum flowed freely, and a large group of drunken hiders was loudly singing bawdy verses from "Looloo Girl."

"Double the picket guards tonight," he suddenly decided. He pulled the makings from his fob pocket and built a cigarette. Then he squatted on his rowels to grab a glowing stick from the nearest fire. He lit the cigarette with it.

"Aw, hell," Patch said, "them Innuns today wasn't nothin' but small potatoes. No need to fret. Besides, Cheyenne won't attack at night."

"Never mind what you've been told. A man can piss down your back and tell you it's raining. It's still piss. I said double the guards."

"Hell, you're the boss. But we got enough guns 'n' ammo with us to wipe out the entire goddamn Sioux and Cheyenne nations combined."

Myers said, "The numbers don't always matter. I was a dragoon in Big Bat Pourrier's unit, we fought Lakota Sioux at Wolf Mountain. We cracked ten-thousand caps in one battle and never killed a hostile."

"Don't matter, boss. God is a white man." Patch's fanatical eyes glowed even brighter in the firelight. "The trumpet of Jericho is a-blowin' the last halleluah. The red vermin ain't got a chance, no more than the buff."

Using the Always Star to the north as a fixed reference, Touch the Sky led his three companions across the vast and silent distance toward the enemy camp.

They tethered their mounts in lush, knee-high grass well back from the camp. Each time fear or doubt tried to weaken his resolve, Touch the Sky only had to remember Uncle Pte lying rotten and swollen in the glaring sun. Arrow Keeper had taught him that the needless slaughter of Maiyun's gifts threw the entire harmony of nature off, and could only end in tragedy for the *Shaiyena* people.

Even so, the four bucks agreed to avoid unnecessary killing after dark. Dying violently at night was a bad death leading to eternal torment; a warrior of honor could not lightly inflict such a horrible fate even on an enemy. So Touch the Sky was forced to lead his men in a detour after he spotted the first picket outpost.

They soon learned that several of these posts ringed the camp. Each was made up of three men, at least one always awake at all times. As he led his band wide around them, Touch the Sky watched a sentry with a torch wander out to examine the ground in the area. The young Cheyenne realized: the guards had been ordered to watch for prints, too, in case they missed other signs of infiltration.

Touch the Sky gathered the others. In a whisper, he instructed them to walk on their heels to avoid leaving prints. Soon they had a crude mind picture of the camp, and he had formed his plan.

"See, over there past that big fire? They have strung a rope corral for their remounts. Dull

Knife, Bear Tooth. You must slip past their herd guards and throat-slash as many mules and horses as you can. Then return to our own mounts, but do not wait for us. Ride back to camp."

He reached out in the darkness to place his hand on Little Horse's muscle-corded body. "Brother, do you see the long wagon beside that tent?"

Little Horse nodded. His features were ghostly in the silver-white moonlight.

"Do you recognize those dark wooden kegs?"

Again Little Horse nodded. He had seen them when Touch the Sky had sighted the line through for the railroad workers, had also seen them on Wes Munro's keelboat. It was black powder: enough to blow that wagon, and any nearby, into a pile of punk and shavings.

"We are going to slip in and give the Yellow Eyes a surprise. We will light up their camp and turn the night into day. Their animals will think the Wendigo has them."

Dull Knife and Bear Tooth set off, angling toward the rope corral. Using knee-deep buffalo grass as cover, Touch the Sky and Little Horse began low-crawling toward the lone wagon. They had nearly reached their goal when unexpected voices suddenly froze them where they lay.

"Aw, don't hand me that barrel of crap, hoss. Ain't no muckety-muck opry singer gunna let *you* drop her linen, you ugly buzzard."

"Doggone my buckskins if I didn't poke that li'l heifer! She was a Frenchie, got real sociable-like when I got her lickered up."

"In a pig's ass! You ain't even been *near* St. Louis, let alone in a opry house there."

"Was so!"

"Horseshit!"

Another few seconds and the two arguing men would step on Touch the Sky! Not only would he be forced to kill at night, creating bad medicine for this mission—if even one of those men sounded a warning, all four braves were as good as dead.

Touch the Sky's knife was clutched tight in his fist. Now the men were only a heartbeat away from walking right over him. His heart pulsed in his palms; sweat trickled through his scalp like scurrying insects. He tensed his muscles for action.

Abruptly, an angry, high-pitched rattling noise sounded in the grass nearby. The footsteps halted.

"It's a goddamn rattlesnake," one of the hiders said.

"Let's plug the sonofabitch."

"Leave it alone. It's too dark. I ain't lookin' to die of snakebite."

Again the noise sounded, and now Touch the Sky realized: Little Horse was making the noise! Touch the Sky had almost forgotten that the men in his friend's clan took great pride in their ability to imitate animal sounds.

Once the palefaces had angled wide, the two braves worked quickly.

Touch the Sky gripped one of the powder kegs and set it on the ground beneath the open tailgate of the wagon. With his knife he pried loose the wooden plug at the top. Then he shook a long line of powder out onto the ground. When the makeshift fuse was ready, he returned the open keg to the ground under the wagon. He spilled more powder loose and laid the open keg in it so it would ignite.

Occasionally, as the two friends worked, they heard a horse nicker from the rope corral. The animals were becoming more and more agitated, and Touch the Sky knew the throat-slashing must be proceeding well—the scent of blood was clearly in the air, upsetting the living animals. The rowdy noise from camp covered the sound, but Dull Knife and Bear Tooth were taking too long. Touch the Sky hoped they would be mounted and escaping by the time that wagon went up.

"Ready, brother?" he whispered to Little Horse.

"Make the sky rain fire, buck!"

Touch the Sky removed his flint and steel from the possibles bag on his sash. He struck sparks only once, and instantly the powder was snapping and sparking, flames racing toward the wagon.

"Make tracks, Cheyenne!" he told Little Horse, even as both warriors, not bothering to cover down now, raced at full speed back toward their ponies.

A few heartbeats later, the sky did indeed rain fire.

A fast, hollow *whoomping* sound was followed by a cracking explosion that stung Touch the

Sky's ears. He felt the force of the blast at his back, hot as animal breath, suddenly saw everything around him lit up as if by lightning. Just before he and Little Horse reached the tethered ponies, he saw Dull Knife and Bear Tooth racing to join them. Dozens of dead horses and mules lay everywhere.

Dead silence followed the explosion. The two braves reached the ponies, hastily untethered their mounts. They also untethered their companions' ponies, holding them at the ready until they could join them.

But Bear Tooth, running behind Dull Knife, never made it. The first shots from camp rang out, blood blossomed from Bear Tooth's right leg as a huge buffalo ball tore his knee out and dropped him as if he'd been pole-axed.

Little Horse started to race back to help him. But Touch the Sky, suddenly feeling the awful responsibility of leadership, caught him by the arm.

"Give it up, brother! Bear Tooth is a dead man, and so are you if you attempt to save him!"

Despite the frustration of leaving a fellow Cheyenne to fall into enemy hands, Little Horse knew his friend spoke straight-arrow. Already a tide of heavily armed whites was converging on the fallen brave. And even now bullets whined past their ears.

The success of the raid muted by this terrible loss, the three Cheyennes leaped onto their ponies and pointed their bridles west toward their camp.

Buffalo Hiders

*   *   *

The torture session lasted long into the night. Sid Myers had ordered a tourniquet applied to the wounded Cheyenne's leg—not to help him, but merely to keep Bear Tooth alive so he could suffer.

"The rest are out there listening," Myers told Patch Orrick and Ace Ludlow. "Let them red vermin know what's in store for them, too."

"*Hail*, yes!" Ace said gleefully. "I'll make that-air red arab sing a tune 'n' that's a fack!"

Ace, Patch, and several others took turns. Knives were heated until the blades glowed red-hot, then laid against the prisoner's bare skin until the smell of singed meat stained the air. They laid rifles against his skull and fired them. The noise shattered his eardrums, the powder flash burned the skin and hair off his head. They broke his fingers one by one, poured boiling water onto his genitals.

Despite Bear Tooth's stoic resolve to die like a Cheyenne, scream after hideous scream rent the dark fabric of the night.

Finally, when the Cheyenne was on the verge of losing consciousness for good, Myers called a halt to the torture.

"Let's finish it and turn in for the night," he said. "Our Cheyenne friends had a good time tonight playing with gun powder. So let's give their game back to them in spades!"

Patch Orrick grinned, his fire-and-brimstone eyes gleaming in the moonlight, when his boss explained the plan. Myers untied the curved powder horn on his sash. He bent over the gasping Cheyenne and roughly jerked his head back. The men gathered around him broke into approving grins and shouts when their leader carefully shook a good measure of black powder into each of the brave's nostrils.

Then he pulled a sulphur match from his pocket and struck it on his coarse leather chaps. The rest of the hiders loosed a cheer as he bent down and ignited the powder, blowing the Cheyenne's skull into a dozen fragments like a clay jar.

Chapter Six

Sounds traveled far across the open plains, especially at night. Touch the Sky and his comrades did indeed hear Bear Tooth's hideous screams of pain—just as the hiders intended.

Usually it was the Indian way to boast after a victory, but now the three Cheyennes maintained a grim silence as they rode. Each of them was deeply troubled. A brave comrade even now was dying a hard and unclean death. There was little to celebrate.

Still, the bold raid had been successful at launching the all-important war of nerves—Touch the Sky kept reminding himself of this. And the importance of this new battle to stop the hiders could not be overrated. Even so, and though not one brave blamed Touch the Sky, he felt the sting of Bear Tooth's death greatly.

"Brother," he said to Little Horse as they rode up out of a long, moonlit draw, "Arrow Keeper always advises us to look before we wade in. I should have taken more time to plan this thing right. Bear Tooth and Dull Knife should have been ready to ride when that wagon went up."

Little Horse shook his head. "Arrow Keeper gives sound advice. But sometimes a thing must be done quickly, before we can pick it up and examine it thoroughly. This was a good strike. We have hit our enemy in their very den. Before he was captured, Bear Tooth killed many ponies and mules."

"And even now," Touch the Sky said with bitter anger at himself, "he suffers from the white dogs' torture."

"He does, if he is not dead by now. But brother, how often have *you* endured torture for your tribe? I once spent a night high up in a tree, watching Henry Lagace and his whiskey traders pile red-hot rocks on you. You, too, screamed. But not once did you cooperate by telling them where the rest of us were hidden. Now you are a leader, buck. Now the weight of responsibility lies heavy across your shoulders. But do not forget, it might have been you who were caught tonight instead of Bear Tooth."

"Little Horse speaks straight," Dull Knife said. "Bear Tooth is my clan brother. He is a warrior, his eyes were open to the dangers. More than once he told me he hoped he would meet his death while locked in battle with our tribe's enemies. It appears he got his wish."

Still, it was hard, and all three braves knew it.

Buffalo Hiders

Bear Tooth's squaw, Sun Woman, had recently borne his first son. Never would he bounce that child on his knee, never sing its praises in the doorway of his clan lodge when his son killed his first eagle with a bow and arrow.

"What next, brother?" Little Horse asked as they pushed on under a star-shot sky.

"Buck, I could easier grasp a badger by the tail than answer that. We cannot attack in any force. All we can do is nip at their sides like wolves worrying a wounded bear. But we have our swift ponies. We cannot stop the killing once the Yellow Eyes find Uncle Pte. But perhaps we can make it difficult for them to find the herds."

"I cannot pick these words up. What do you mean to say?"

"Only this. The whites must have herd-scouts out. If we can find out where the hunters are going before they get there, perhaps we can also make sure the herd is gone when the killers arrive."

Dull Knife nodded in the moonlight. "I have ears for this. With a little warning, Uncle Pte can move quickly."

"I am for it too," Little Horse said. "We have only to send out good trackers to locate their scouts."

"But a thing troubles me," Dull Knife said. "So far they have been content to let us come to them. What happens when these white hiders decide to rout *us*? If they ride against us as one, in this flat grazing country, how will we stand and hold? And yet, where could we run?"

Touch the Sky had already shed much brain sweat trying to solve that thorny problem. Earlier he had claimed that following the spirit path would not win this battle. Nonetheless, Little Horse was watching him closely now. His best friend sensed what the others did not: that the hand of the Great Medicine Man was in everything, that Touch the Sky always watched for a sign from that hand.

But Little Horse knew it was not his friend's way to boast and make grand promises of divine protection, as some shamans did. Touch the Sky's next words proved this.

"Buck, if a warrior stops to think on all the ways he might go under, he will lose the courage for even a war whoop. We are the fighting Cheyenne of the Northern Plains! If the fight comes to us and we are trapped, it will be one bullet for one enemy. When bullets are gone, arrows will fly. When our quivers are empty, we will break out our clubs and knives and lances. When they drop our ponies, we will use them for breastworks and fight on. The color of death is on our faces. The battle is never over until the last Cheyenne brave is dead."

But despite these brave words, Touch the Sky shared Dull Knife's fear. After all, the point of this mission was not to prove how bravely a Cheyenne warrior could die—it was to keep the entire tribe alive by saving the all-important buffalo. Coup feathers and scalps were useless if there were no people left to admire these symbols of courage.

Once again they stopped briefly while Little

Horse dismounted and turned to listen carefully behind them. He had the keenest ears in the tribe. He knelt and placed one ear just above the ground for a long time, listening. The sturdy little brave also placed several fingertips lightly against the ground to sense movement.

"They are not pursuing us," he said finally. "They are content to take their anger out on Bear Tooth."

"Then we have not yet angered them enough," Touch the Sky said. "But count upon it, the time is coming when they surely *will* ride after us. Now mount your pony, brother, and let us return to our camp. Tomorrow is another day. We will make these hair-faced slaughterers pay, and pay dearly, for the right to kill Uncle Pte."

Next day the hair-faced hiders *did* ride out.

Sentries from the Cheyenne camp spotted them on the horizon around mid-morning: a group of perhaps 30 well-armed hunters, leading a pack horse. After a sentry raced back to report this ominous advance, Touch the Sky called a hasty council.

"Brothers, our first chance for a battle is now approaching. But do we fight on their terms? Do we mount against them or hold from pits and try to lure them closer so their long rifles are no advantage? Or do we fight them in a retreating battle?"

"Is this even a good time to fight?" Tangle Hair said. He still wore the slouch beaver hat he had snatched during the first raid on the whites' camp, though several coup feathers now adorned it. Likewise, Little Horse wore his stolen saber in his sash.

"And what if this advancing party is only a feint?" said Ute Killer, the brave whose pony had been shot. "These hair faces are clever at deception, the rest may converge from our flanks."

"I have ears for all this," Touch the Sky said. "I am as keen to fight as the next brave. But I too feel we must keep the battle on our terms. If we dig pits here, now, they may soon become our graves."

Little Horse, Dull Knife, and the rest nodded agreement. But even as they counseled, another sentry rode in with more news: The hiders had stopped while still well out on the plains. They dumped something on the ground, then turned back toward their camp.

Touch the Sky and the rest already knew what it was they had dumped. But nothing was said. His mouth a grim, determined slit, Touch the Sky rode out with Little Horse to investigate.

The object lay in the lush buffalo grass, wrapped in a piece of tattered canvas. The two friends dismounted in silence and hobbled their ponies. Then each knelt and grabbed one end of the canvas, unwrapping it.

Bear Tooth's mutilated remains tumbled out into the grass. Touch the Sky felt a flash of ice, a burst of fire, a prickling rush of blood to his face as the shock hit him.

The head—what little remained—was shattered beyond all recognition, the body scarred and ravaged beyond belief. Both braves held their faces impassive in the Indian way, refusing to let their sadness and rage creep up into their faces.

Out of respect, Touch the Sky had refused to desecrate his enemy's flag. But look what *they* had done to Bear Tooth. He felt no shame when hot tears momentarily filmed his eyes— Little Horse, too, was rapidly blinking back tears.

But the moment passed. Once again Touch the Sky made his heart a stone with no soft place left in it. Thus, it was ready for the hard battle to come, where every soft place would only be one more spot for his enemy to wound.

"We will return to the thickets and fashion a travois," he said. "We will send two braves to take Bear Tooth's body back."

He and Little Horse automatically made the cut-off sign, as one did when speaking of the dead.

"If this was meant to make us show the white feather and flee," Little Horse said bitterly, "these Yellow Eyes are confusing the Cheyenne with the Poncas. Fresh white scalps will soon dangle from my clout, brother. I swear this thing. These men lower than a pig's afterbirth have no place to hide from Cheyenne wrath. If they be in breastworks, we will drive them out, long rifles or no."

"More of us will die too," Touch the Sky said. "More of us will look like *this* before it is over. But I swear by the four directions of the wind, before we have done with them, these whites will

do the hurt dance while we smear our bodies
with their blood!"

"I'll teach these red vermin *never* to come
between a dog and his meat!"
Sid Myers stood just past the perimeter of the
huge buffalo camp, staring out across the open
vastness to the west. Huge, low-hanging black
clouds were piling up like boulders. Ace Ludlow
stood on his left, Patch Orrick on his right. They
were all watching for the volunteers to return
from delivering the body.

"Dog and his meat," Ace repeated. "That's
a fack."

"Shut your gob, you simple shit," Myers said,
his voice tight with irritation. Behind the three
men, the camp was crawling with activity. Men
stood over huge iron pots, boiling their clothes
to kill the fleas and lice. Others played poker
or stood in line outside the mess tent, drinking, smoking, occasionally brawling. Some were
tending to their weapons, readying them for the
next slaughter session with the buffalo herds.

"Why'n't we just ride out and do for 'em?"
Patch said. "Give 'em a lick of Old Testament
glory."

"That's you," Myers said. "Do everything full-
bore. You think there ain't more Injuns waiting
for us to do just that? The Cheyenne tribe loves
to send out decoy groups to lure enemies out
of their camp, divide them up. Your problem is
you don't credit the red man with any brains.
Just cuz they're killers and thieves don't mean
they're stupid."

"Stupid!" Ace repeated. "Me 'n' the buff, *hail* yes!"

"Already," Myers said, "they've cost us horses and mules. That's the second wagon we've lost. And now I'll have to send men to Red Shale for more powder."

"Well, if we ain't gunna put at 'em, what do we do? Let them keep naming the game?"

Myers shook his head. "A fish always looks bigger underwater. So far the Injuns been in their element. But once they lose control of this fight, we've gut-hooked our fish. And they're about to lose control."

"Here comes Jimmy!" Ace said. "*Hail* yes, that's a fack!"

Myers and Patch both looked where Ace pointed. Out across the brown vastness a rider approached. They recognized the big, 17-hand claybank of Jimmy Longtree, the half-Ute, half-white buffalo scout they had hired on in Red Shale. Myers had sent him to the northwest in search of buffalo herds.

"Plenty buff at Greasy Grass," he announced as his horse trotted up. "Jimmy doan spot no herd. But he seen plenty buffalo bird, you bet."

Myers' gruff, serious face broke into a rare smile at this good news. He turned to Patch.

"Pass the word. We break camp in the morning. I want every swinging peeder ready to move out at sun-up. We got buff to kill."

"Buff to kill!" Ace repeated elatedly. "*Hail* yes, that's a fack! Gunna get me a juicy sumbitchen liver!"

Patch Orrick's fire-and-brimstone eyes were

glowing with the promise of another blood-letting. Myers stepped upwind of his stinking chaps.

"If them Cheyenne was mad before," Patch said, a smile tugging at his unshaven lips, "wait'll they see a *big* herd wiped out. They'll be ready to harrow hell then, by God!"

A hush fell over Gray Thunder's Cheyenne camp when Ute Killer and another brave rode in with Bear Tooth's body.

The camp crier had already announced their arrival, riding up and down the camp streets and shouting the news over and over. So most of the people had already congregated in the clearing before the council lodge. Old Arrow Keeper was on hand, along with Chief Gray Thunder; Lone Bear, leader of the Bull Whip troopers; Spotted Tail, leader of the Bow Strings; Black Elk and Wolf Who Hunts Smiling.

Honey Eater, her lower lip caught tightly between her teeth, edged closer through the crowd. When she caught sight of the body, unrecognizable now, pity roiled her insides. This emotion was followed immediately by a burning anger at the injustice of such treatment—and by a cold fear for Touch the Sky's safety. Would he be the next to return to camp in this condition? Was he even still alive?

Her eyes met Black Elk's, and he read the worry in her face, knew full well whom she was worried about. His dangerous scowl sent a cool feather of fear down her spine.

Suddenly a hideous wail assailed their ears:

76

Buffalo Hiders

Bear Tooth's bride, Sun Woman, had just learned of the death of her brave. In a pattern too familiar to the long-suffering Cheyennes, the women of her clan gathered in a protective circle around her. For the next few sleeps she would be watched closely to make sure she did not snatch up a weapon and kill herself in her grief. Her cries cut into Honey Eater's heart like lance points.

Ute Killer made his report, beginning with the astounding shot which had killed his pony at such a great distance. When he had finished describing the nighttime raid and the torture of Bear Tooth, collective rage hung over the camp like a dense fog.

Spotted Tail, troop leader of the Bow String soldier society, addressed Chief Gray Thunder.

"Father! Of course this thing will be discussed in council. But I am for sending some more of my Bow Strings out now to reinforce Touch the Sky and the others. You have heard Ute Killer's words. As things stand now, they are just enough to be seen by their enemy, but not enough to engage them in battle. We have sent Touch the Sky into combat with his hands tied."

"This idea would be scanned," Black Elk said. "We cannot spare warriors. Has Spotted Tail already forgotten what happened the last time we left our women and children and elders poorly protected in their camp? Those same Comanches and Kiowas who stole our people then now threaten us again."

"Fathers and brothers!" Wolf Who Hunts Smiling said. He had been about to ride out when Ute Killer arrived. Now he held his pure black pony by her hackamore. His pony, like his cousin Black Elk's, had the black and red flannel streamers of the Bull Whip troop tied to her tail.

"May the white dogs who did this thing to Bear Tooth die choking in the yellow vomit! Only, think on this thing. Does it not seem curious that these white hiders attack at the very time when we are unable to divide our numbers? One might almost believe that they perhaps had a spy among us, one who could tell them the perfect time to strike at Uncle Pte."

Honey Eater understood immediately what Wolf Who Hunts Smiling was hinting at. So did most of the others. It was no secret that he now called Touch the Sky by the name White Man Runs Him. Now some scowled at this familiar suggestion that Touch the Sky secretly played the dog for white men. Others slowly nodded, thinking about it. This Touch the Sky, they asked themselves, why did he always end up in the middle of trouble—trouble which always seemed to pit the red man against the white?

Honey Eater's anger was immense. Again Touch the Sky's enemies were conspiring against him, even as he put his life on the line for his people. She almost spoke up, despite the taboo against women taking part in discussions of tribe business. But Black Elk would accuse her of trying to make him a squaw in front of his clan and troop brothers. Nor would things go any easier for Touch the Sky.

It was Black Elk who spoke up now. "My

cousin is right to raise this question! An Indian who speaks out of both sides of his mouth is a serious threat to his people. It is not good enough to say, this warrior, he is marked for visions, his medicine is strong, therefore he is above suspicion. Better to ask, does he speak the white man's tongue?"

This was well said, and Wolf Who Hunts Smiling immediately followed this trail. "Look here at our brother, Bear Tooth! He died unclean at the hands of our worst enemies. Did he have to die this way, or was he sacrificed by this Touch the Sky, this 'seeker of visions'? Is this tall stranger a false Cheyenne secretly counseling with whites? Was Bear Tooth's life the price of their combined treachery, the sham by which Touch the Sky makes all of us *believe* he is at war with the very people he secretly plays the dog for?"

Many were nodding, others grumbled in protest. But it was Arrow Keeper who spoke up.

"Wolf Who Hunts Smiling often accuses me of being a soft brain in my frosted years. So perhaps I missed our chief's announcement. I was not aware that a council had been called to attack Touch the Sky."

"Perhaps one *should* be," Wolf Who Hunts Smiling said defiantly. His swift-as-minnow eyes mocked the old medicine man.

"If so," Arrow Keeper replied calmly, "you will not be allowed to speak. Everyone here knows that you have chaffed like a sulking child ever since the Council of Forty stripped you of your coup feathers. Everyone also knows why they were taken from you. You spoke in a wolf bark against Touch the Sky and caused him to swing from the pole when he was innocent."

"You dote on him, old one, because he claims to be a visionary. You are a fool. He has played the fox with you and many others."

"Yes," Black Elk said, his fierce dark eyes meeting those of Honey Eater. "He has played the fox with many. But all foxing ends when a blade sent between the fourth and fifth rib goes straight to the heart."

Black Elk lifted his hand to the bone handle of his knife. He smiled when the color drained from his wife's face.

Chapter Seven

Once again the Cheyenne's fate would depend on superior speed and mobility.

A flank guard from Touch the Sky's camp had seen the halfbreed scout return to the hiders' camp. The guard was careful to note the exact direction from which the scout arrived—from the northeast and the Valley of the Greasy Grass. The next morning, Touch the Sky and Little Horse watched the hiders break camp. They rode out in the same direction from which the scout had reported.

"Count upon it, brother," Little Horse said, watching their enemy ride out. "Their plans are nothing but bloody. They are off to the slaughter."

Touch the Sky nodded. He sat his high-spirited mare. The two braves had found rare shelter behind a lone stand of wind-twisted cottonwoods.

"As sure as the earth we live on, brother. Now we must read their sign even before they make it. We must reach Uncle Pte before they do."

"This thing would be done carefully," Little Horse said. "True, the whites are encumbered by their wagons and their equipment. Their very numbers, which force us to such caution, also limit their speed. But you see how vast this part of our range is. The herds could be anywhere. If we miscalculate the paleface arrival point, even a little, our effort may prove worthless."

"I have already wrestled with this. This morning, early, I sent Tangle Hair out to trace that scout's back trail. He is marking sign for us even now. Wherever that scout rode, these hunters are riding."

Little Horse nodded, liking this. He still wore his captured saber. But he had given it the Indian touch, tying eagle-tail feathers and pieces of enemy scalps to the hilt. "Then let us ride back. We must make sure Uncle Pte is long gone by the time these death merchants arrive."

"Ride we will, and soon. But first, before we leave the river thickets of our present camp, we will make fires of cedar and sage and sweet grass."

Again Little Horse nodded, understanding immediately. It was not good enough to simply reach the buffalo. They must get close enough to "point" them as a herd and stampede them in the right direction. This meant somehow getting around the buffalo's keen sense of smell.

Buffalo Hiders

Smoking their moccasins, clothing, and skin over wood and grass fires would help disguise the human smell.

Touch the Sky was acutely aware of the need for this precaution. During his first hunt, he had stupidly gotten upwind of the buffalo. The herd had scattered, wasting hours of work and enraging Black Elk and the others. Even today, his enemies still accused him of having the stink on him for life, that he created bad medicine for the hunt.

For a moment, before they rode back to join their comrades, Little Horse read some of these thoughts in his friend's face.

"Brother, your enemies within the tribe have forced you to constant vigilance. In camp, I have seen how you never rest without a tree at your back. But I have noticed another thing, too. I have noticed how more and more of the people now speak openly *for* you, too. 'This Touch the Sky,' they are saying out loud, 'he is straight-arrow Cheyenne to the quick, and no man to trifle with.'

"To a man, all of Spotted Tail's Bow Strings consider you a warrior worthy to wear the Medicine Hat into battle. They will never forget how you fought at Tongue River, or the day you rallied the unblooded warriors and saved our women and children from Kiowas and Comanches. They would ride into battle beside you, buck, and take the bullets meant for you."

Despite his current dejection, Touch the Sky could not deny these important words. At one time he was without any friends in the tribe except old Arrow Keeper and Honey Eater. Even Little Horse had once been hostile, if not exactly his enemy. Now some of the old grandmothers and young girls sang about his deeds in songs that would endure until the last Cheyenne on earth crossed over. Now some of the tribe's best warriors openly carried their pipes to his tipi, while even his worst enemies admitted he fought like ten men.

"A battle is brewing," Little Horse said. "A battle within our tribe. Even now the sides are forming. Your enemies grow more determined even as more of your supporters speak up. A crisis is coming to its head, many in the tribe will be forced to choose between leaders. It will be a choice, not only to select our leaders. But a hard choice about our tribe's destiny, about who we are as a people and what it is we believe."

These prophetic words, coming from a warrior as taciturn and practical as Little Horse, moved Touch the Sky deeply.

"I knew you were gifted with a keen ear and eye. But I did not know, brother," he said quietly, "that you kept such a close watch on things yet to pass."

A smile briefly divided Little Horse's otherwise impassive face. "In truth, Cheyenne, I do not. These are things Arrow Keeper said to me while you were off scouting for Caleb Riley and the other white miners. But because it *was* Arrow Keeper, I take the vision as truth."

"If Arrow Keeper spoke these things," Touch the Sky agreed, "they will pass. But for now, brother, let us put the distant future in our parfleches. It is also Arrow Keeper who says, 'Wake to the living world, or sing your death song!'"

He pointed below, where the huge formation of hiders moved with the ungainly yet awesome precision of an army.

"The present battle will keep us busy enough. Now, ride hard, and hope we reach Uncle Pte before these hair-faced murderers do."

Sid 'Long Rifle' Myers pushed his mount hard, riding him with his rowels when the cavalry-trained sorrel started wanting water. Once Myers had fixed on a target, he brooked interference from neither man nor beast. There would be water near the buffalo. The horses could drink, the men eat, after the slaughter.

Flanked by Ace and Patch, he led the long columns across Wyoming country as God-awful open and flat as any he knew. Small rivers were frequent, and the Shoshone River was big enough to provide some temporary table-land and limestone cliffs. But mostly it was open and vast, a sea of lush grass dotted with occasional wild flowers and scrub trees. If there was beauty in any of it, it was lost on Myers. For him, familiarity had long ago bred contempt. He was busy calculating profits from the sale of buffalo hides and pickled buffalo tongue.

Despite their fearsome firepower, Myers had ordered flank riders out. These Northern tribes, they were crazy bastards once they painted for war. They got all jacked up on fasts and trance-dances, and the next thing a man knew, his top-knot was gone.

He reined in his mount for a moment, glancing all around him. "You got an eye out for the buffalo birds?" he shouted over to Patch.

"Boss, does okra make your piss stink? I ain't never missed 'em yet." To emphasize his point, he reached up and slid the black eyepatch into place over his left eye. "I shoot better with one eye than any 20 of them lubbers behind us."

"That ol' okra, she'll made your piss stink, *hail* yes," Ace said. "That's a fack!"

"I swan, that bastard gets wilder every day," Patch said. "You trust him with a gun?"

"Why'n't you set it to music?" Myers said impatiently. "When he quits shooting plumb, that's when I'll take his guns."

Myers cast one last, long look around. Thank God this wasn't hill country or that damned Southwest canyon land. Surprise attacks by daylight were out of the question. That English-speaking Cheyenne buck had sworn to destroy them. Well, Myers agreed he had a set of oysters on him—that was bold as anything when his trio charged through camp right under their noses. But though boldness and impulse and luck could make a warrior great, they could not work forever. Not on the open plains.

Abruptly, Myers heaved his great, shaggy bulk straighter in the saddle. The stock of his Hawken protruded from one saddle scabbard, his Volcanic repeater from the other. He could feel the weight of his big Navy Colt on his thigh. He clucked at his horse, and the killing legion moved out. Swirling, dark clouds boiled in the sky behind them, casting a huge storm shadow over the plains and all who lived there.

"Here comes the wrath of Jehova!" Patch Orrick shouted. He raised his octagonal-barreled Hawken high in the air, and behind them the hiders loosed a cheer. "Buffalo and red heathens beware, the trumpet's a-blowin'!"

Tangle Hair had done a good job of marking the halfbreed scout's trail. Touch the Sky pushed his braves hard, unencumbered by wagons, remounts, or provisions. Despite the urgency, he signaled frequent halts so their ponies could drink. He knew they would soon be sorely tested.

The Cheyennes did not waste daylight by making cooking fires. As they rode, they chewed on pemmican and dried plums from their legging sashes. Each time he cast his eye around at his companions, Touch the Sky could not help contrasting their small number to that virtual army of cold-blooded marksmen.

"Have you spotted the birds yet?" he asked Little Horse and Dull Knife yet again. And again they shook their heads. But now the grass was getting higher, more lush, and the rivers spawned more coarse-barked cottonwoods. These might attract the great, shaggy beasts. It was shedding season—this made the buffalo itch constantly, and they loved to rub up against the cottonwoods for relief.

While their ponies drank from a rill, Little Horse knelt to place his fingertips on the ground.

"They are moving steadily, brother, if not swiftly. We are still well ahead."

"But recall," Touch the Sky said, "we do not merely need to reach the herd first. We must get them bunched and pointed, the stampede underway, before the hiders come into killing range."

"And *we* must have time to escape too," Dull Knife said. "Once they see who has cost them Uncle Pte's robes, they will turn their rifles on us with a vengeance."

Touch the Sky and Little Horse exchanged a brief glance, saying nothing to this. For much remained to be done in a brief time—and escaping from the white men was last on the list, when time might well be all used up.

The halfbreed scout named Jimmy Longtree had changed mounts, slept for a few hours, then ridden right back out on Myers' orders.

He frowned when, several miles out from camp, he spotted a small mound of dirt which had not been made by an animal.

Someone was marking his trail.

He spotted sign several times after that: small mounds of dirt, grass twisted to point the way, blazes in the bark of cottonwoods and oaks. Advancing under cover of thickets near the Weeping Woman Creek, he finally spotted the lone Cheyenne.

Jimmy recognized his tribe instantly from the style of the braid. He never once considered killing the brave. True, the Cheyenne had become the Ute's enemy ever since the Ute men began cooperating with blue-bloused soldiers. But the big mountain Indian truly respected Cheyenne warriors. Like their fierce cousins the Sioux, they were no braves to trifle with.

Why risk his life to please white chiefs, Jimmy thought. This Cheyenne scout was not his problem, but the palefaces'. Besides, if he simply killed the Cheyenne, he would have no bargaining power with Myers. However, if he *watched* him, gathering information, that information could be traded for whiskey and coffee and the fine white man's tobacco.

Jimmy let the scout build a good lead again. Then he nudged his big claybank out from the cover of the thickets, resuming the long trek across the vastness of the plains.

"Brothers!" Little Horse shouted, reading sun signals as they were flashed with a fragment of mirror by Tangle Hair out ahead. "Tangle Hair has spotted the buffalo birds! Soon we reach the herd!"

Using the familiar hand-and-arm signals of the hunt, Touch the Sky formed his warriors into two narrow columns for this final leg of the ride. Keeping the wind in their faces, they closed in on the grassy river valley.

They crested a long rise, and Touch the Sky spotted the buffalo birds—tens of thousands of them, feeding off the ticks of an equal number of buffalo. The Cheyennes slowed to a trot and rode closer, until the buffalo themselves came into view.

Touch the Sky's heart sank when he saw

how widely fanned-out the herd was. Could his braves ever bunch them in time? He wasted no time agonizing over it: Now came a startling, impressive display of Cheyenne hunting and riding skill.

Tangle Hair joined them. No commands were necessary—the braves knew what needed to be done and the best way to do it. Lashing their ponies to full speed, becoming one with their mounts, they veered from the strict column formations. One by one, the braves expertly fanned out and took up outriding positions, ringing the huge herd.

They clung low over the necks of their ponies, minimizing the human shapes. Uncle Pte had bad eyesight. At first, pony shapes could be mistaken for young buffaloes. Inexorably, the braves closed their ring tighter like a noose, nudging the buffalo into a smaller and smaller formation. But soon enough the lead bulls smelled the human scent, and the stampede bellows sounded.

Again Touch the Sky marvelled at how the call of an enraged bull sounded like that of an enraged grizzly. And as the stampede began, the hardest job began for the Indians—pointing the herd out of the valley and onto the open plains.

Now no one bothered with hiding. Braves sat up on horseback and raised their yipping war cry. Ammunition was too scarce to waste. But the Cheyennes managed to raise an infernal racket of shouts, whoops, and whistles.

For one long and tense moment, Touch the

Sky was sure they would lose control of the herd. The vast formation surged and swelled, the middle threatening to break down into chaos. Bulls roared, cows lowed, calves bawled in panic; ponies nickered and snorted, hooves thundered on the ground. The Cheyennes added to the din with their savage cries.

Touch the Sky felt himself being pressed in from all sides as huge buffalo closed in on his pony. Time and again an enraged bull dropped its head and tried to gore the spirited blood mare; time and again she danced out of harm's way just in the nick of time.

The ground heaved and trembled beneath him. Huge divots of dirt and grass tore loose and flew up into his face. Then, quick as a blink, his pony stumbled, and suddenly Touch the Sky was hurled headlong to the ground under thousands of pounding hooves!

The blood recovered herself before being trampled. But Touch the Sky, flat on his back under a wave of stampeding bison, had nowhere to run nor even time to stand. It was all happening quickly, too quickly. And then Little Horse rode in from the left flank, Tangle Hair from the right. Desperately, Little Horse held his war lance across so that Tangle Hair could grip the stone tip.

Touch the Sky had only a split-second to react. He reached up with both hands, caught the lance as it flashed overhead, and was lifted from the ground even as a stinking bull leaped onto him. One horn grazed the sole of an elkskin moccasin as he was whisked to safety.

In a feat of combined riding skill that rivaled the best Comanche riding tricks, Little Horse and Tangle Hair rode side by side, matched step for step, their timing perfect as the stampede carried them along. Meantime, Touch the Sky somehow swung up onto Little Horse's pony.

"Brother," Little Horse greeted him in a show of exaggerated calm, "it would appear that today is not a good day for you to die."

After that harrowing moment, Maiyun chose to smile on them. The stampeding buffalo not only picked up speed, but began bunching tighter and tighter. Then it was easy to point them out of the valley. The sick and lame animals were forced to the front of the herd with the calves. Those who couldn't keep up would become food for the wolves.

The last of the herd had disappeared to the west before the white hiders entered the valley.

Chapter Eight

Jimmy Longtree fell silent and assumed the blank face he always used around whites and other invaders who wore shoes. This white man called 'Long Rifle' was clearly angry—dangerously so. *All* whites were dangerous. Best to take what they gave you and leave them alone.

"How many Cheyennes?" Myers demanded. "Plenty Cheyenne?"

Jimmy shook his head. "Plenty buff, you bet. But Jimmy doan see no plenty Cheyenne. Maybe squad."

Myers nodded. Jimmy, who had first scouted for soldiers, habitually used Army units to express the size of an enemy group.

Myers looked at Patch. "Maybe you was right after all to feel frisky about attacking them and getting it over with. It don't sound like they got a big war party in reserve. If they do, where was they when the herd was stampeded? You heard Jimmy say they damn near lost control of it."

"That's what I been sayin' right along. There ain't that many of 'em. But the longer we hang fire, the longer we give them. Time to join with Sioux, 'Rapaho, and whatever the hell other raggedy-assed Innuns read their smoke sign. You let these Plains tribes get all worked up to a trance, they'll grease our bones with war paint. I say it's time to fish or cut bait."

This was the first time Patch had even hinted at feeling any possible danger to the hiders. Now Myers knew they could no longer treat these Cheyenne raiders as mere piss-ants. They were about to become a serious threat to the morale of his men.

"We'll cook their hash," he said. "You can chisel that in granite. Take an order back to the group leaders. I want a search-and-kill party. Pick 50 of our prime marksmen. Provision them light for fast riding. Fresh horses with good grain rations. You and me will lead them ourselves, make sure this thing gets done right."

"*Now* you're talkin'!" Patch said. "We'll do the hurt dance on them-air red Arabs."

"Fish or cut bait," Ace said. "*Hail* yes! Sons-abitchen Injuns gunna grease ol' Patch's bones with war paint, that's a fack! Ol' stinky chaps is goin' under!"

"If that crazy bastard don't shut his gob," Patch said, his hands working into big, meaty fists, "I'll snap his skinny neck like a chicken's."

"Never mind wasting a war face on that simple

bastard. You know what to do. Those goddamn Cheyennes just as good as robbed us. I don't take it lightly when somebody keeps me from gettin' my living. And you tell the men. The one who kills that tall, English-speaking buck will be spending a pouch full of double-eagle gold coins when this hunt is over."

Only one full sleep after herding Uncle Pte to safety, the signal was flashed from a sentry's mirror: *Enemies right on us, soon the attack!*

Touch the Sky's band had sheltered in the rolling hills west of the Shoshone River. Now, as word of the attack came, he quickly scaled a tall tree. Gazing to the northeast, he soon spotted the riders.

"Brothers!" he called down to Little Horse and the others. "Now we are in for sport! These riders are at least twice our number. They have no wagons or remounts or supplies to slow them down. All they pack are weapons and the desire to put us under."

"We have seen what their long rifles can do," Little Horse said. "If we shelter here, they will simply wait until we must hunt for food. Our ponies are grazed and well-rested. I say we take to the plains. I say it is time for these hair-faced invaders to taste a Cheyenne battle."

Despite the fear churning his stomach, Touch the Sky grinned briefly at his friend's bold words. Below him, at least half the warriors loosed a war cry when Little Horse quit speaking. His friend was one of the most respected braves in the tribe—slow to lift a hand in anger, but once his enemy came at him, he never paused to calculate the odds. He was a warrior, so living or dying was not his focus in battle. Only fighting the good fight counted, and winning it for his tribe.

"Little Horse speaks straight!" Tangle Hair said as Touch the Sky began to climb down. "Our ponies are the best on the plains. Let us show these spur-wearing dogs who invented the cavalry!"

Another brave broke into a battle song as they quickly rigged and checked their ponies. Lances, clubs, axes, rifles were secured where they would be quick to hand. The braves checked one another's sashes and quivers and sheaths to make sure they were secure. Those with rifles verified that they were loaded and primed. Each brave silently touched the totem inside his medicine bag, drawing strength for the fight.

The fighting spirit was strong, in part because of the recent success at steering Uncle Pte clear of the killers. But Little Horse eased up beside Touch the Sky as the tall youth rigged his mare.

"Brother, we are horse warriors and will count on our ponies once again. This time they are ready. But if this fox-and-chicken battle keeps on, we and our ponies will soon be caught in poor fettle. We cannot simply keep striking and running, striking and running. Nor can we resort to ground fighting, as the Apaches prefer. We need to poke quick and hard at their vitals."

Touch the Sky nodded, his mouth a grim, determined slit. His friend was right. Soon they would have to force this fever to its crisis. And already the nubbin of an idea was forming in Touch the Sky's mind—an idea inspired by his near miss yesterday, when he had almost been trampled to a paste beneath the stampeding buffalo.

But now it was still too early to speak of this plan.

"As usual, brother," he answered his friend, "you have truth firmly by the tail. We have no plan and another hard battle ahead. But only think, we have saved one herd. And while these pale dogs are nipping at us, they are diverted from further killing of Uncle Pte. We are not just running. We are also leading the hair-faces by their bridles."

By the time the Cheyennes broke from the hills, fleeing onto the plains to the south, the whites could be spotted from the ground.

"Do not forget, we are already in range of their weapons," Touch the Sky said. "We will ride out in two groups and attempt to divide them. Little Horse, pick your men and ride to the right of those hills. I will lead the rest around on the left."

Suddenly, as he quit speaking, Touch the Sky recalled something the dead Chief Yellow Bear had told him—told him in a prophetic medicine vision which had convinced the youth of his destiny.

"Place these words in your sashes!" he added now. "When all seems lost, *become your enemy!*"

He loosed a war whoop. The two battle groups

surged forward, enemy bullets already nipping at their heels.

As Touch the Sky had hoped, their enemy divided to pursue both groups. Thus the battle turned into a classic Cheyenne fight. Those destined to survive the day's bloody engagement would give it the name that would be often repeated in clan circles: the Buffalo Battle.

It came down, once again, to the ponies, which were the center of their warrior culture. Every spring Cheyennes paid tribute to the all-important ponies by dedicating a "gift horse" to Maiyun, the Good Supernatural. Now, as their mounts once again became their principal hope in the struggle between life and death, this almost fanatical devotion to horses paid off.

The ponies responded as if they were mere extensions of their riders' will. The braves formed narrow columns to minimize targets. Warriors with rifles rode closest to the hiders. As the first bullets began whining past their ears, they nudged their ponies into amazing evasive-riding patterns—patterns too intricate for a marksman to anticipate by "leading" his target.

Despite these precautions, a lucky shot caught the hindquarters of a pony belonging to a brave named First Son. Even before First Son quit rolling and bouncing on the ground, two braves had dropped back to help him. One took him up on his pony, the other quickly stripped the rigging off the fallen mount.

The whites, too, had powerful horses. They

bore down on the Cheyennes, sharing a single-minded instinct—like fierce wolves closing on a blood scent.

Firing their double-charged Hawkens from horseback did not allow them the luxury of careful, pinpoint aiming. But the balls struck whatever they hit with a powerful impact. One shot shattered a rawhide shield, another struck a warrior's wooden gunstock and splintered it.

The whites narrowed the distance. Suddenly a cry rose from the rear of Touch the Sky's group. A warrior flew from his pony, blood spuming from a fatal hit to his neck.

Another volley of lead whanged past, a pony nickered piteously and went down with a fatal wound.

Touch the Sky could not see Little Horse's group, cut off by the hills. But the number of rifle shots from that direction told him his friend was up against similar treatment.

Now, as the pressure to save his men mounted, Touch the Sky felt himself hardening to the challenge. The retreating battle was going badly. But at least they had succeeded in dividing the enemy force.

Now it was time to follow Chief Yellow Bear's advice.

Touch the Sky glanced into the chamber of his percussion-action Sharps and made sure he had a cap and ball behind the gate. Then, with a double thrust overhead of his red-streamered lance, he abruptly ended the retreat by turning it into a charge.

As one, the braves pulled back on their buffalo-hair bridles. In a collective movement unrivaled by the best show ponies, the Cheyenne mounts seemed to whirl and reverse course without missing a step. While the ponies executed their finest battle moves, their Indian lords performed theirs.

Lances came up to the ready, seeking warm vitals.

Arrows were notched, rifles aimed, braves bouncing with perilous ease on their ponies.

Stone skull-crackers were raised for the single crushing blow which could send a man across the Great Divide forever.

"One bullet, one enemy!" Touch the Sky shouted. It was the famous rallying cry which they had learned from their bullet-hoarding Sioux cousins. "Hi-ya, hii-*ya!*"

As one man, the Northern Cheyenne hurtled toward their surprised enemies, outnumbered, but with their screaming war faces marked with the color of death.

So far Sid Myers and Patch Orrick were enjoying this little chase. Each man had led a group in pursuit when the Indians had divided. Myers chased the tall buck, Patch his sturdy little friend, who now taunted them by waving his stolen saber.

Patch had slid his eyepatch into place to cover his nervous left eye. Now, despite his ungainly form on horseback, despite the hasty snap-shots he was forced to, he had killed one brave and dropped a pony.

Myers, too, was enjoying the plinking. Hooking his left leg around his saddlehorn as was his habit, he lay his Hawken across it to steady his aim. He had wounded one Cheyenne and dropped a buckskin pony for the carrion birds.

"*Hail* yes!" Ace Ludlow screamed from the right flank. "*Hail* yes, *hail* yes, *hail* yes!" Each time he said 'hail,' he snapped off a round from his Volcanic repeater. Despite his soft brain and the smaller powder charge, his aim was good. His bullets were taking more effect as the hiders steadily closed the gap.

Myers lost sight of Patch and the others as they disappeared behind that big, double-humped hill. He was steadying his rifle across his chaps, about to squeeze off another shot, when one of his men suddenly hollered a warning.

Myers glanced up, and what he saw made his blood seem to flow backwards.

The tall Cheyenne buck was bearing right the hell down on him, mounting an attack!

"Christ!"

Myers never even had time to lift his leg off the saddle. He saw the man to his left fly from the saddle, an arrow buried three inches into one eye socket. Then the tall buck's rifle leaped.

His shot was plumb. But the bullet he had sent toward his enemy's guts grazed the sturdy barrel of the Hawken first and was deflected. Myers felt a white-hot tongue lick his cheek. Then, only an eyeblink later, each group had passed the other.

Little Horse, too, had whirled his braves in a surprise counterattack. Now both Cheyenne battle leaders merged their warriors. They escaped in the same direction from which they had come.

Myers, fingering his bloody cheek, watched Patch and his men charge out behind the fleeing Cheyennes. The fire-and-brimstone sheen in Patch's eyes told Myers that he, too, had been bamboozled by the Cheyenne trick.

"Don't sit there scratchin' your hinders!" Myers shouted to his dumbfounded men. "We got Indians to kill. Put at 'em! And don't forget, a pouch of gold double-eagles to any swinging peeder who kills that big one!"

The reverse attack had been highly effective for both groups of Cheyenne warriors. Several hiders had been killed or wounded, the others clearly unnerved.

Touch the Sky had cursed his luck when his shot failed to kill their big, bearlike leader—a hard target to miss. Instead of unstringing the white man's nerves, the close encounter with death only seemed to make him more dogged in the pursuit. Now, as the white hiders again began to close the distance, Touch the Sky felt his desperation growing.

The reverse had not broken their enemy's will to fight. Now, without the element of surprise, it could not be used again. Nor could the Cheyenne ponies keep up their exhausting evasive-riding tactics.

"Brother!" Little Horse pointed out ahead. They were approaching a creek swollen with spring runoff.

Touch the Sky nodded, understanding Little

Horse's thinking. If a stand must be made, best to clear the creek and then turn on their enemy. With luck, the Cheyennes could get into position and fire while the hiders were vulnerable during the crossing.

Using hand signals, they told the others what to do. No one bothered fording the creek—each rider urged his mount over in a reckless leap, a few of the ponies struggling for footing on the opposite bank.

Touch the Sky and Little Horse dropped aside to cover their men as they crossed. Now, as the white hunters closed in, the two Cheyennes slowed them down with frugally spaced, but expertly aimed, shots.

Then, disaster.

Two braves had attempted to leap the creek at the same moment. Their ponies collided in mid-air and tumbled into the rain-swollen water. One broke its leg. Now it blocked the very spot where the rest must land.

At least a dozen braves had still not crossed. As they fanned out in search of alternate spots to cross, the bloodlusting palefaces raised a kill cry and surged forward.

Everything after that happened with the timeless confusion Touch the Sky had learned to associate with close combat.

A withering line of fire killed Little Horse's pony. Realizing they were trapped where they stood, Touch the Sky ripped the rigging off his own pony and slapped her rump hard, sending her across the creek. Then, his eyes meeting Little Horse's in a wordless signal, both braves leaped behind the dead pony and used it for a breastwork.

The bold-charging whites had already killed another Cheyenne buck as he prepared to leap the creek. Now Touch the Sky expended another precious bullet, dropping a hider from the saddle. Little Horse's scattergun roared, roared again, and two hiders set up a chorus of screams as their faces were torn off.

Bullets rained in on them, so thick that Little Horse's dead pony jerked and twisted as if flies were still pestering it in death. Their long rifles empty, the two fighting Cheyenne youths dropped them and slid fire-hardened arrows from their quivers. One after another they launched deadly volleys. Hiders screamed in agony as an impossible number of arrows flew in on them like giant, vindictive porcupine quivers. They pierced hats, arms, legs, faces, the flanks of their horses.

Their desperate stand had so far purchased the time needed for the remaining Cheyenne to cross. Now, pressed shoulder to shoulder, Touch the Sky and Little Horse made a final stand for their own lives.

Their comrades on the opposite bank were forced to find cover and, at first, could lay down little return fire. Touch the Sky launched his final arrow, burying it deep in a hider's groin. As Little Horse, too, emptied his quiver, the whites surged forward to finish them off.

Touch the Sky wrenched the battle axe from his rigging. He whirled it overhead twice, released it, watched it slice deep into the chest of an attacker. Now his knife was in his fist, now flying through the air. It caught a hider in the belly and knocked him sideways on his mount.

A bullet creased Touch the Sky's forehead, hot blood streamed into his eyes. A hider raised his rifle to fire and Little Horse sent his war lance sliding into him. More riders were suddenly on top of them, a confusing swirl of limbs and weapons, curses and shouts. Touch the Sky grabbed his Sharps by the muzzle and used it as a war club, knocking whites from the saddle and clubbing them senseless. Little Horse, screaming the war cry, pulled a hair-face from his mount and sliced his throat open before he hit the ground.

This incredible display rallied their comrades to a battle frenzy, even as the hair-faces drew up short—these two braves were crazy-dangerous grizzly bears! Cursing them, their leader shouted to retreat as the return fire from across the creek began to heat up.

For a long moment, the paleface in the filthy woollen chaps trained his one visible eye on Touch the Sky. He thrust his rifle defiantly into the sky.

"It's comin' down to me 'n' you, red nigger! I aim to plant a buffalo ball in your lights!"

And then the badly shaken whites retreated as more Cheyennes returned fire. The fiercest battle in Touch the Sky's memory was over, though no clear winner had emerged. But the war against the hiders had just begun.

Chapter Nine

Touch the Sky's war party was in ragged shape. They had dead braves to prepare for the final journey to the Land of Ghosts; several men were seriously wounded; others were without ponies or short on provisions. As Little Horse had reminded him, a battle could quickly turn into a slaughter under these conditions.

"Brother," his friend said one sleep after the bloody battle, "I know it galls you to lose track of these white hiders. It galls me too. But I see nothing else for it. We must return to Gray Thunder's camp, at least briefly."

Reluctant though he was to admit this, Touch the Sky nodded. "I have ears for this, buck. Returning now will embolden the *Mah-ish-ta-shi-da*. They will feel certain they scared us off. But we cannot fight on spirit alone. Your pony is dead. And the wounded need better care than we can give in this makeshift camp."

The survivors of the bloody Buffalo Battle made up a war-weary, exhausted column. But they held their heads high as they rode back. After all, had they not survived fierce combat against a well-armed enemy who vastly outnumbered them? They had earned the right to boast to lesser men. Beside a lone, unnamed runoff creek on the Wyoming plains, they had covered the Cheyenne people in glory. And the two bucks leading them, both mounted on that fine blood mare—this Touch the Sky and Little Horse. Had they not performed as magnificently as sky-warriors whose deeds are immortalized in the stars? The very telling of it made some of them feel gooseflesh.

Never would the enemy survivors speak lightly of Cheyenne warriors! Even now Little Horse and Touch the Sky bore the scarlet smears where they had rubbed their bodies with enemy blood. Even now, as they rode, excited braves described how the two friends had stood side by side and repelled a mounted attack using knives and battle axes, swinging empty rifles as clubs.

The reception at Gray Thunder's camp, however, was far from a hero's welcome.

As usual, as soon as sentries spotted them, the camp crier raced throughout the village, announcing their arrival. But the people did not all enthusiastically flock out to greet them, as was the custom when a war party rode in. Only old Arrow Keeper, Spotted Tail of the Bowstring troopers, and a few wives and clan relatives, anxious to learn the fate of their braves, did so. There were also a few elders, the old grandparents who had been saved from Kiowas and Comanches when Touch the Sky rallied the junior warriors to victory. They were among his most loyal supporters. But few had real influence with the Council of Forty.

This reception did not surprise Touch the Sky. Wolf Who Hunts Smiling, Black Elk, and the rest of his enemies had been spreading their lies and rumors, chipping away at the chinks of his credibility. *Only look*, their smug faces seemed to say as the warriors rode in. *What an inglorious return for the mighty warrior!* And indeed, Touch the Sky admitted, there was a bad look to it.

"The people are confused," old Arrow Keeper told him on the first night of their return.

The two friends sat as they often used to, cross-legged beside the cooking tripod in front of Arrow Keeper's tipi. They had just shared a succulent elk steak dripping with kidney fat.

"They are confused because, by your own report, our enemy is not defeated. Yet, Bear Tooth"—here Arrow Keeper made the cut-off sign—"was carried in dead and savagely mauled. Now come several more dead braves. All of this dying with no victory gives credence to the lies your enemies are spreading."

Arrow Keeper paused to sip from a horn cup filled with hot yarrow tea. In the leaping orange flames, his face was as wrinkled and ridged as an old apple core.

"For your enemies have cleverly planted this suggestion. They say you are deliberately letting the whites destroy our herds for a share in the grisly profits. Meantime, you pretend to fight them. They say these hiders are the same hair-faces who built the path for an iron horse across our lands, the same ones you helped before."

Though he held his face impassive in the Indian way, Touch the Sky's tone was bitter when he answered.

"*Letting* the whites destroy our herds? Father, only a few sleeps ago this 'white man's dog' was but a cat's whisker away from death at white hands. These hiders are as different from Caleb Riley's miners as pigs are from eagles. If I hear even one brave accuse me of playing the dog for these hiders, I swear by the four directions I *will* sully the Arrows."

Arrow Keeper studied his young friend closely in the firelight. How the youth had aged, filled out, hardened during his few winters with the tribe! Yes, this was indeed the young warrior of Arrow Keeper's great vision at Medicine Lake.

At first, the old shaman had doubted. This untutored youth named Matthew Hanchon still had worn shoes and offered his hand to Indians! But then the tall, broad-shouldered Cheyenne had eventually proved he was indeed the long-lost son of the great Cheyenne Chief Running Antelope. The day would come when this lone warrior would lead the entire *Shaiyena* nation in their greatest victory. But until that day arrived, what suffering and torment he must endure!

"You have been patient," Arrow Keeper finally said. "Your enemies have humiliated you, attempted to kill you. They have poisoned your name with the tribe, and even now they plot against you. Through such treachery they have quit all claim to any honor. Buck, you have clear cause to kill them. But even so, I refuse to sanction this letting of tribal blood. Do you, my shaman apprentice, understand why?"

Stubbornly, Touch the Sky shook his head. "No, father, I do not! You yourself told me that even a shaman must keep his weapons to hand. Of course it is a serious thing for a Cheyenne to shed another Cheyenne's blood. But you saw them beat me senseless with their bullwhips! You saw me swing from the pole because of their lies. They have loosed a grizzly on me, set Pawnee upon me, taken shots at me from ambush, 'mistaken' me for an elk and fired upon me. They call me a white man's dog, Woman Face, and White Man Runs Him. Now, every time I spot a pony with Bull Whip streamers on its tail, I must grab a weapon. Now I sleep like a rabbit, starting up at the first snap of a twig or screech of an owl.

"And father, if all this were not enough misery for one lifetime, they have torn my life asunder from that of the only woman I love. Honey Eater is the soul of my medicine bag. How long have I been back in camp? Yet I dare not lay eyes on her for fear Black Elk will kill her. You yourself once said I would be forced to kill my enemies within the tribe."

"And so you will. But only when there is no other way out. Only when they have forced your hand. For though it is true you have clear enough cause to kill, you must understand. You are now a leader, buck, and you will be a bigger Indian yet! The younger warriors look up to you, they copy you. A leader cannot be tarnished. For if gold will rust, what then will mere iron do? You are marking the way for your tribe, upholding the ancient Cheyenne law-ways which give us our being as a people."

These words flew straight-arrow. Touch the Sky examined them a long time, for Arrow Keeper's words were always important. Then he nodded.

"As you say, father. I will do everything in my power to avoid bloodshed. But let any one of them actually bridge the gap against me, and *I* will finish the kill."

Arrow Keeper approved this with a single nod. "Fair enough, buck. A man must defend himself. And remember this. You are training to be a shaman. As you lock horns with these buffalo hiders, look to your shaman's sense, too, not just your weapons. For every battle road, there is also a spirit road."

Touch the Sky's warriors wasted no time in preparing to return to the battle.

Little Horse and a few others cut fresh ponies from the common herd. Weapons were repaired and cleaned, legging sashes stuffed with pemmican, jerked buffalo, dried fruit. Recent scouting reports verified that the Comanche named Big Tree was still leading a war party north from the Blanco Canyon. Until their intentions were known, no more braves could be spared to assist Touch the Sky.

Early on the morning when they were due to ride out, Little Horse stopped outside his friend's tipi.

"Brother! Lift the flap, I would speak with you."

Touch the Sky stepped outside. He had been busy shaping new arrows from green pine, and now he held a half-finished arrow in one hand.

Little Horse said, "Let us take a walk together, buck."

Touch the Sky's eyebrows met in curiosity. "Walk? To where?"

"Down by the river, brother. A little bird has come to me. Now I have a thing to show you. I think it will interest you."

Touch the Sky knew his friend well enough to see that Little Horse was barely restraining a smile. But neither was Little Horse one to trifle with a man. Touch the Sky poked his curiosity into his parfleche and followed his friend.

They were crossing the central camp clearing, heading for the grassy, sloping bank of the Powder. A familiar voice drew them up short.

"Look here, brother! Little Horse wears a long knife, just like the blue-bloused cowards who killed my father!"

The speaker was Wolf Who Hunts Smiling. He and Swift Canoe were seated in front of the hide-covered lodge of the Bull Whip soldier society.

"Yes, Panther Clan," Swift Canoe said. "And did you notice how Tangle Hair now wears a white man's hat?"

"I did, brother, I certainly did. It would seem

that White Man Runs Him is not content to carry the white man's stink on him for life. He must also convert our Cheyenne men into *Mah-ish-ta-shi-da*."

"This is the way it is with hair faces. They are not content until they have nailed shoes on their horses and taught the red man to answer roll calls. They value a turncoat Indian, for such as these make their job easier."

"You two jays," Touch the Sky said. "Jabber all you will. Cowards spend words freely, as drunken whites spend coins. A true warrior talks with deeds, not words."

"Well, and these are not true warriors," Little Horse put in. He stared at Swift Canoe until the other man looked away. "These are loud, blustering bullies who place themselves ahead of their tribe. Such as they are a disgrace to our people."

"Perhaps," Wolf Who Hunts Smiling said, "my blade will soon bluster its way into your guts."

Little Horse bit back his reply. Touch the Sky watched him glance toward the river, as if reminding himself of something.

"If we had crossed over once for every threat from you," Touch the Sky said, "we would still be busy dying. But that is the way with young girls. They have talk where *men* have courage."

This was a sure hit at the young Indian's pride. As livid rage contorted Wolf Who Hunts Smiling's face, Touch the Sky gripped his friend by one elbow and pulled him toward the river.

"You call *me* a girl?" Wolf Who Hunts Smiling raged behind them.

"Surely," Touch the Sky said, flashing a brief smile as he gave his enemy a dose of his own favorite medicine. "Why, look now how the squaw's face screws up in anger, showing her feelings for all to see. Why, is her little chin quivering?"

"Perhaps," Little Horse said, "our young girl is even now bleeding from her belly mouth? Perhaps she needs to visit the Once A Month Lodge?"

Both Cheyennes threw back their heads and roared in open contempt as Wolf Who Hunts Smiling flushed scarlet with rage. But when he went for his knife, the humor left Touch the Sky's eyes.

"Think carefully on this thing, buck. I will tell you what I just swore to Arrow Keeper. Any man may call me anything, or even brandish his weapons at me. I am indifferent. But let him once move to bridge the gap, and *Death* is the name that is on me!"

Swift Canoe laid a hand on his friend's shoulder. Wisely, Wolf Who Hunts Smiling sheathed his weapon. Touch the Sky and Little Horse together would be like fighting ten men.

"Gloat, White Man Runs Him! Enjoy playing the big Indian as you strut about with charcoal on your face, pretending to hunt white men. More and more in the tribe are beginning to understand how well you play the fox. Now, even as these hiders destroy Uncle Pte, they are secretly paying you to help them. If I speak bent words, where are white scalps to match for our dead braves? You told the council you saved a herd. But you only drove it into the bead sights of the hiders, you make-believe Cheyenne!"

Despite the satisfaction of goading Wolf Who Hunts Smiling, Touch the Sky's spirits were at their lowest in a long time. It had been easier to mock his enemy than it would be to clear his name. And now he understood: Anything short of a victory over the hiders would be seen as treachery on his part. His enemies had cleverly trapped him.

Now, as he followed Little Horse toward a secluded copse well past camp, he had lost his curiosity to know what was afoot. Then he spotted the youth called Two Twists, standing guard at a bend in the path.

"Now, brother," Little Horse said, glancing all about them, "you are safe. Black Elk has ridden out to scout the situation with the Comanche. He will not return for hours. True, his spies are everywhere. But we have eluded them all. A little bird flew to me and requested this meeting. She is over there. Go to her now, but remember, listen for the owl hoot if danger approaches."

A moment later, Little Horse had disappeared into a thicket. Touch the Sky, his heart pulsing in his palms, stepped through the wall of reeds Little Horse had indicated.

And found Honey Eater on the other side, waiting for him.

"You have come," she said, and her relief was so great that huge tears formed on her eyelids.

Even before he remembered to breathe, Touch the Sky reached out and took her in his arms.

She felt fragile as a bird through the thin blue calico of her dress. The fresh white columbine braided through her hair was as fragrant as her honey-tinted skin. She felt warm and soft against the bare skin of his chest, except for the hard points of her breasts.

Touch the Sky tasted her hair, the back of her neck, lifted her chin and surprised her by pressing his mouth against hers. She had never been kissed before—red men did not kiss their women. But her body learned the desire for it quickly, her lips opening under his, her tongue probing against his.

Reluctantly, as if sensing that she had better stop now while she could, Honey Eater pushed him back a little.

"Black Elk constantly accuses me of lying with you. I would keep him a liar, though in truth it is out of no love or respect for him."

Touch the Sky only nodded, still not trusting his voice.

"I know it is dangerous to meet like this. But Touch the Sky, when Little Horse came to me, I begged him to arrange it! We cannot stay long. When Black Elk's troop brothers realize I am not visiting with my aunt Sharp Nosed Woman, they will search for me. Oh, Cheyenne, I am so afraid! This time Black Elk and his cousin are determined to turn the people against you. I am here to beg you, be careful! I know you face a deadly enemy out on the plains. But these enemies in your own tribe, they now see that you are meant to become a leader. Their own treacherous plans will not abide such a fate."

Buffalo Hiders

"You have eyes to see, little one, sharp ears to hear. They are for me, and time sets with the sun. Arrow Keeper says my destiny is fixed. I am set to endure what I cannot avoid. I confess, the hardest hurt of all is seeing how Black Elk has ruined your life—the life you should be spending with me."

His words flew straight to the quick of her feeling, and tears sprang before she could stop them.

"I heard you announce one time," she said, "before the entire tribe, that *you* had a husband's right concerning me, not Black Elk. They were bold words."

"They were," he said, meeting her eyes. "And no one bucked them."

"No, no one did." Modestly, she looked at the grassy bank beneath them. But her next words were anything but modest.

"You were right. You *do* have a husband's right! I must go now before I am missed. But Touch the Sky, I have thought long and hard on this thing. I accept what is wrong, according to Cheyenne way, and I accept what is demanded by my love. By *our* love."

Now she met his eyes again and placed one soft hand against his cheek. "Touch the Sky, it will not be easy. But I will suffer the risk if you will. If you send for me, I will come to you and lie with you as your wife."

Chapter Ten

Reoutfitted, their numbers even smaller now, Touch the Sky's war party again rode out into the belly of the beast.

Before his secret meeting with Honey Eater, Touch the Sky had seriously doubted his ability to continue leading this impossible mission. Now, having heard this proud daughter of a great chief vow that she would sacrifice even her good name for him, his courage and fighting spirit had been born anew. He would match her courage with his own!

But love her though he might, the immediate issue now was the safety of his warriors. The bloody massacre of his men could not continue. No battle leader worth the name ever forgot his obligation to keep his men alive if at all possible. So more and more now, as they rode east toward the imaginary line the whites called the 100th meridian, Touch the Sky recalled Arrow Keeper's hint: *For every battle road, there is also a spirit road.*

A plan had begun forming. But Touch the Sky knew a harder task lay before him first. Despite the loyalty his men felt toward him, the rumor back at camp was taking its toll: the rumor that he only pretended to be at war with these whites. He needed to send yet another clear and dramatic signal back to the main camp. He also needed to serve once again as an example of courage to inspire his men to supreme effort. It was individual effort that Indians admired most. He would watch for the opportunity. And the moment would surely come.

If Little Horse was curious to know more about his recent meeting with Honey Eater, his manner hid it well. In this, as in most matters, Little Horse stuck to his belief that men of few words seldom had to take any back. He spent much time observing the ways of his new ginger mustang. During the infrequent pauses, he rode out onto the flanks and watched for sign of danger. He sensed that Touch the Sky was forming a plan—and by necessity, a desperate plan.

As they approached the beginning of the vast buffalo ranges, the Black Hills were visible on the far horizon. No commands were issued. But the braves voluntarily fell silent and contemplative, studying the darkly forested hills at the center of their world. But their minds wandered to fears closer at hand.

By returning to the site of the Buffalo Battle,

they easily picked up the trail of the hiders. It bore due north, toward a northern buffalo range known simply as Dunes: a flat stretch of short-grass prairie bordered by mile after unbroken mile of steep-sided sand dunes.

"Brother," Little Horse said soon after the hiders' new course had been determined. "This thing troubles me. Have you heard why the white hunters prefer the Dunes over other ranges?"

Touch the Sky only nodded, his mouth set in its grim, determined slit.

"I have heard, brother. Old Knobby, the mountain man, was first to tell me this thing. Once I believed that this could not be true, that even hair-faces were not so lazy and ruthless. But since the discovery of Uncle Pte in his boneyard on the plains, I know these hiders are without even a gnat's breath of honor."

"Honor? I thank Maiyun that some whites value this word, brother. Tangle Hair fought at the Washita. He saw a Bluecoat soldier killed by his own eagle chief after he refused to fire on our unarmed women and children. Tangle Hair buried him after the battle, and sang his courage in a song. And to this day no man in his clan will fire on any Bluecoat who does not fire on a Cheyenne first."

"I have heard him speak of this thing. But these hiders, they make no distinction between Indian and animal. It is all in a day's butchering, to them."

For the second time, a flock of sparrow hawks flew by overhead, coming from the direction they were riding. Touch the Sky and Little

Horse exchanged long glances. Such sightings were considered important warnings. For after all, any Cheyenne knew that sparrow hawks fled from humans.

"Ace," Myers said, "you dumb galoot, get your face away from that barrel! That's a 12-pound howitzer. You think we blew that Cheyenne's head apart? This'll blow what's left of your brains clean to the Superstition Mountains."

"Shee-*yit!*" Ace said, backing his face away from the gun's muzzle. "I'm a dumb galoot, that's a fack!"

"That's pure-dee fact," Patch agreed. " 'Dumb' is the range you graze in."

"Patch, when the hell you gonna learn to leave it alone? His brain's gone soft, you might as well talk Latin to a goddamn mule. Now hand me them matches."

Myers wrinkled his face in disgust as he got downwind of Patch's filthy woollen chaps. They stank of old blood and old meals, of all the animal and human guts he had wiped off his blade onto them.

Patch handed his boss a bunch of matches wrapped in oilskin to protect them from water. Down below them, a good-sized herd of buffalo was strung out in a grazing pattern. Normally, stampeding such a strung-out herd would ensure that many got away. But just behind these animals lay the steep sand dunes which gave this area its name.

"All right," Myers said. "The men form a skirmish line at wide intervals and hold it. They can ride forward a little, but *don't* let 'em into the dunes! Lead'll be thick there, and besides, I've seen that loose sand break a horse's leg quick."

Patch nodded. He slid his eyepatch into place, removed a wad of bee's wax from his possibles bag and stuffed some in each ear—the incredible din, like his nervous eye, distracted his aim. Myers marvelled again that such a high-strung shooter could be so deadly. But once he focused on a target, Patch was unerring. Comanches were the natural jockeys of the Plains, yet he could knock one from the saddle at 1500 yards, knock his horse down from over a mile distant.

While Patch rode back to convey the orders to the group leaders, Ace suddenly caught Myers' eye.

"Ol' Patch, he gunna lose his top-knot 'n' that's a fack!"

Myers, who was a tad superstitious, half believed the stories about soft-brains predicting the future. Seeing the serious look on Ace instead of his usual half-wit's leer, Myers felt flies stirring in his belly.

"When?"

"Pretty damn quick, *hail* yes!"

"How 'bout me? What d'you see about me?"

Ace threw his head back and roared with laughter. "Shee-*yit!* I see plenty buff, that's a fack!"

Myers decided he liked that answer. Plenty of buffalo meant plenty of money. He watched now until Patch gave the signal: all the hunters were locked and loaded and in position.

Buffalo Hiders

Myers struck a match on the rough wood of the wagon. He held it over the touch hole. A moment later nearly a pound of tightly wadded black powder ignited.

The shell itself killed several buffalo and wounded several more. But the incredible report of the howitzer, still booming out across the dunes, instantly panicked the herd. Intent only on running in the opposite direction of these invaders, the lead bulls charged straight into the steep-sided sand dunes.

The mighty crack from the howitzer, still well out of sight ahead of them, made the fine hairs on Touch the Sky's neck stand up.

Almost immediately after the big gun fired, the first angry bellows were joined by the precise cracks from the Hawkens and Volcanic repeaters. Touch the Sky's braves dug sharp heels into their ponies. Though they constantly looked to Touch the Sky, Little Horse, and the other lead warriors, the braves rode in no formation. Indians depended on speed and daring, not disciplined battle formations.

They broke over a long rise, and the terrible scene unfolded before them like a Navajo sand painting.

The hiders were making easy sport of it, most not even bothering to mount their horses. For the buffalo had trapped themselves, hooves virtually useless in the loose sand. They tripped, one piling on top of another. Two-hundred rifles cracked relentlessly; when one barrel heated up, the hiders would simply grab their second rifles.

The whites, engrossed in the slaughter, were slow to look behind them. Touch the Sky sized the situation up in one good look. The main thing he noticed was the wide intervals between the marksmen, how their line stretched away far to the west. Clearly they had not expected Indian attacks today. That wide interval might be his only chance.

It was easy to spot the filthy woollen chaps of the hair-face with the religious-crazy eyes—the one who had challenged him at the Buffalo Battle.

Touch the Sky dipped his lance twice, telling the others to hold. Then, not even debating the wisdom of it, he urged his pony to a gallop. He bore straight down on the spot where Patch Orrick stood in a wide stance, firing offhand into his sector of the herd.

Touch the Sky had closed the distance by perhaps another 100 yards when someone shouted a warning to Orrick. He turned, and his uncovered eye spotted the attacking Indian.

Calmly, a confident smile dividing his face, he dropped into a prone position and lay the repeater aside. He picked up his big Hawken gun and dug his left elbow into the dirt, laying the gun across it.

Touch the Sky spoke words into his pony's ear and she abruptly went into her evasive-riding pattern. She side-jumped, swerved, crow-hopped, yet somehow continued forward at amazing speed.

Patch still had plenty of time. He fired, missed, reloaded.

Fired, missed, reloaded.

A bead of sweat rolled out from under his eyepatch. Now all the men around him were watching intently, as were the Cheyennes.

Again he fired, missed. And now there *wasn't* so damn much time.

He tossed the Hawken aside and picked up the Volcanic. This was a 30-shooter, and he could get off every shot quickly. That was just about how much time he had before this crazy-assed redskin overran him.

Like angry hornets, bullets began whirring past Touch the Sky's ears. Even while his pony danced for her life, he swung from flank to flank, peeking out from below her neck to keep track of the distance. All that was visible most of the time was one of his feet.

He winced when a round took off the tip of one of his moccasins, when another creased his scalp. Then, incredibly, he was almost on top of his enemy.

Touch the Sky swung back on to his pony's back, braced, leaped off in mid-stride. He flew square on top the stinking white man, the impact knocking him hard to the ground and smashing the wind out of him. Without missing a heartbeat. Touch the Sky grabbed the man's filthy hair and yanked it back hard. He held one foot down on the struggling hider's neck, made his quick outline cut.

A moment later, he jerked hard and the scalp snapped free.

Patch Orrick had been scalped alive. And Touch the Sky planned to let him live. A scalped man in their midst would do far more to frighten the rest than a dead man.

Even as Orrick found enough wind to loose a hideous scream of pain, Touch the Sky shoved the bloody scalp into his sash.

He turned to call his pony. And then his heart leaped into his throat when he saw her lying about 20 yards out. Blood pumped from a fatal shot to her skull.

Patch, writhing in agony and shock, was in no condition to threaten him at this moment. But already the men on either side were training their weapons on him. A few Cheyennes were firing back, mostly nuisance shots to keep the whites nervous while Touch the Sky escaped.

But he wasn't escaping. Instead, while the shots increased all around him, he began walking slowly and calmly toward his dead pony.

"That sumbitch is dumber 'n' me!" Ace chortled. "*Look* at the crazy bastard! Shee-*yit!*"

"He's dog meat now!" Myers shouted. "Plug him!"

Still Touch the Sky walked calmly forward. He felt the eyes of Little Horse and every other Cheyenne in his band now fixed on him. What he did now would count forever, and he knew he must keep down the fear of death.

Bullets fanned him, tickled his leggings, whanged by so close and often the air seemed to scream from them. But in a final act of defiant bravery, he knelt amidst the withering fire and removed his dead pony's hair bridle, pretending that nothing dangerous was happening.

It was so brazen that the whites ceased fire

without an order from Myers. More than one of them began to laugh and whistle and cheer at the sheer audacity of this savage. Either he had one hell of a set of stones on him, or he was as tangle-brained as Ace.

But to a man, the Cheyennes understood what their battle leader had just done. He had not only counted coup and scalped an enemy for all to see, but this purely symbolic act of defiant bravery had just put blood in the eyes of every warrior. More important, the delay had given Uncle Pte time to flounder out of the sand dunes and break for the open plains. Even now Myers was cursing his men, telling them that good money was escaping on the hoof.

And then, in the midst of all the confusion, Little Horse had swooped out and pulled his friend up behind him, even as the astounded hiders again opened fire on the Indians.

Chapter Eleven

Cecil McGinnis, one of the group leaders, said, "What was it like, Patch, being scalped?"

"I hear," a hider said, "that it hurts like a sonofabitch."

"Does it really make that noise I hear about?" said another. "That kinder sickenin' noise like bubbles poppin' when the hair is lifted?"

"Katy Christ," Patch said, disgust warring with the pain in his voice. "You sound like a bunch of damn wimmin clucking over a newspaper. Leave me the hell alone now."

He was resting in the tent reserved for the sick, lame, and lazy. One side of the tent was rolled up, and curious onlookers had gathered in a little knot. A hider named Jack Hupenbecker had been a horse doctor for the Army. He had applied a strong-smelling liniment and a linen dressing for Patch Orrick's severe scalp wound.

"Won't be no fleas jumpin' out your hair *now!*" somebody said, and most of the men laughed.

Patch was stretched out on a cot. Now his voice went low and dangerous. "Laugh all you want to. But I'm tellin' you for the last time, leave me in peace. I got a hogleg pistol under this blanket for the next jackass that makes a joke about my hair."

The men slowly dispersed. But one of them called out, "Watch your top-knot, Deadeye!" and another chorus of laughs erupted.

"Scum-sucking bastards," Patch muttered from the cot. "Used to was, *men* come out west. Now it's a bunch a damn titty babies."

Sid Myers had remained behind in the doorway of the tent. His disgust was clear when he spoke.

"You talk the he-bear talk, all right. But lately, when it comes down to the rough weather, you ain't worth a cup of cold piss. Now you're whining like a sickly girl. It ain't Ace I need to get shed of, it's you."

"The hell! You watch, I'll soon be feelin' fit as a ruttin' buck."

"Well, by God, you best start *act*ing like one. Thirty bullets in your weapon, and that naked savage counted coup on you, lifted your dander! Don't you see what this is doing to the men? Started out like a holiday, now quicker 'n' scat we're up to our armpits in shit! They all saw what that upstart buck did to you. You and me are the best shots in this outfit. If Injuns can skin *you*, how do you think they're feeling?"

"Hell, that Cheyenne got lucky, is all, I—"

"Luck didn't have shit to do with it. He whipped you."

"In a pig's ass! I—"

"Shut up," Myers said. "Shut up and listen to me. I want that red bastard killed. Not only killed, but killed hard, and in full view of the men. They've got to see that he's not some kind of untouchable god. Did you hear how some of them actually *cheered* when that savage escaped? This ain't no Robin Hood, it's a goddamn criminal keeping us from making our living. I've doubled the reward for the man who kills him."

"That'll be me," Patch vowed.

"I don't care, so he dies. But meantime, the men have got to have a victory over these Indians. They've got to see them humbled. Jimmy just rode in with some news. There's four Cheyenne bucks riding the foothills of the Eagle Tail Mountains, a hunting party, Jimmy says. I'm taking McGinnis and his group. We're bringing 'em back here. Alive. Only, they won't die so fast as the last one did. We'll put 'em out in plain view for this English-talking showoff to see."

"Wait a day and take me."

"Wait hell. We're burning good daylight as it is. If you ain't off your ass by the time we ride back in, I'm leaving you here."

"I'll be up. I want me a crack at them redskins."

"There's plenty will be taking a crack at them. *You* best concentrate on the one that raised your hair. I got a feeling, next time you two hug, he won't leave air in your lungs."

"I'll cover my own ass. You just remember, Long Rifle. If he *does* plant me, you'll be next on his list."

Because no full warriors could be spared from Gray Thunder's camp, the task of hunting for fresh meat fell to the junior braves.

Two Twists, Lame Deer, Full Quiver, and Goes Ahead were assigned to the area near the Eagle Tails, where antelope herds had been sighted. Buffalo were plentiful, of course. But ancient Cheyenne Hunt Law was strict on the matter of buffalo hunting: It could be done only once a year, and the entire tribe must take part in the hunt.

After two sleeps, constantly on the move, the hunters brought down a handsome antelope buck. They butchered out the parts and packed it onto a travois. Now they were heading back to camp, eyes alert for more game. One antelope would not go far toward easing the hunger of the tribe.

"Brothers," said Full Quiver when they had stopped to water their ponies, "I have noticed a thing. Those who ride for Lone Bear and his Bull Whips are often meeting behind Black Elk's tipi. But somehow, I do not think it is these Kiowas or Comanches they discuss."

Full Quiver carefully avoided Two Twists' eyes. He was tactfully creating the opportunity for Two Twists to speak on this subject. Everyone knew the youth admired Touch the Sky and had done so ever since the outcast warrior had rallied Two Twists and his brother warriors in training in a brilliant defense of the hunt camp. Full Quiver and Lame Deer had both fought in that battle.

Goes Ahead awkwardly stared at the ground. His father was a Bull Whip, as were the men of his clan. The others respected this and knew clan loyalty was strong. So they spoke around him.

Two Twists, so named for his double braid, said, "Count upon it, they are plotting against their own tribe, not enemies from without. And know too that honor is not in the mix. These Whips sully the Arrows as casually as they steal meat from the racks of Bowstring troopers."

Full Quiver nodded. "My father says a few of them are good men. But they are easily led. And Wolf Who Hunts Smiling enjoys playing the leader."

"Yes," Lame Deer said, "even when he is pretending to let Black Elk lead, he in truth leads him about like a child. Black Elk is fierce enough, but he has been knocked hard on the head. And now jealousy has him firmly by the tail."

They were surprised when Goes Ahead spoke up.

"My father is a Whip, all my uncles too. But I am taking my gift arrow to the Bowstrings when my time comes to join a troop. I decided this thing when the Bull Whips beat Touch the Sky during the annual hunt. I am proud to say that my father, though he did not speak up forcefully, was against the whipping."

Two Twists was about to speak when Lame Deer said, "Brothers, look there! I see trouble on the wind."

They looked where he pointed out across the plains. A group of perhaps 20 well-armed riders approached. They were white men, buffalo hunters judging from their clothing and rifles. And their leader, a huge bear of a man with a Navy Colt tied to his thigh, flew a white truce flag.

"I say that flag means nothing," Two Twists said. "If we move now, we still stand a chance of mounting and outriding them."

"I have ears for this," Full Quiver said. "These men do not come to parley. These are the hiders Touch the Sky was sent out to fight. I say we make tracks now!"

But the youths, like their fellow Cheyennes riding with Touch the Sky, had yet to learn about the long-distance power of the double-charged Hawken. The leader of the whites dropped his truce flag, and suddenly his men opened fire against the ponies where they still milled near a wallow. All four went down, dead or dying.

And the young Cheyennes abruptly realized they had nowhere to run, no way to get there if they did. They did have downed ponies for breastworks. But any fight made now would quickly become a slaughter.

"Brothers!" Two Twists shouted. "We can fight to a sure death or take our chances and live to fight later. I say, if we are warriors, we will not choose death until there is nothing else for it. Though it galls me too, *I* say we surrender and watch for our moment. Perhaps they will kill us outright, but what of that? Without ponies out here, they have killed us anyway."

Slowly, one by one, his three companions nodded. Two Twists turned to face the approaching whites. He raised both hands, open and empty, in a gesture of peace.

"Remember, brothers," he said softly even as he made the peace gesture, "our knives are close to hand. If we must fall now, let it be on a white man's bones."

However, Two Twists regretted his decision after the white leader had ridden closer. One glance into the flat-as-stone eyes of the hiders convinced the youth: he and his fellow Cheyennes would soon die a hard death. And their chances of killing any of these frontier hard-cases were slim indeed.

Their huge leader knew a few words of Sioux, though language was hardly necessary. Under heavy guard, the Cheyennes were roughly thrown down and searched, their knives and other weapons seized. A few of the stinking hiders entertained themselves by kicking or punching the prisoners. One kept attempting to light Two Twists' braids with a sulphur match.

But their leader seemed intent on preventing any serious harm to them now. Several times he stopped his men when their horseplay got too rough. But Two Twists was sure he was only saving the Cheyennes for a special purpose.

One of the white men, a skinny man with a perpetual leer, was clearly crazy-by-thunder. He seemed fascinated by Two Twists' braids. Several times he groped for them, but the big leader kept pushing him away.

"Goddamn it, Ace, you simple shit!" he said, the words incomprehensible to Two Twists. "Keep away from them Innuns!"

All hope for escape vanished when the Cheyennes were trussed to white remounts for the journey. They were each drawn down tightly on the horse's back, arms and legs secured under the mount's belly by several loops of strong new rope. They could barely lift their heads to look about them.

After a seemingly endless ride across unbroken plains, they broke into a stretch of cutbank country bordering Bear Creek. The trail narrowed to single file. The prisoners, with absolutely no chance for escape, brought up the rear. All four of their horses were tied to a long lead line; it had been snubbed around the saddlehorn of one of the hiders.

Two Twists brought up the rear. The pain in his ankles and wrists, where the ropes bit into him like rattlesnake fangs, was savage. Only by causing excruciating pain to his neck could he even glance up to see around them.

That's how he spotted the crazy-by-thunder white man, riding silently beside him. The soft-brain leered foolishly when Two Twists met his eye. He had gradually dropped back so that none of the others noticed him. Now he held a sharp-edged Bowie knife in his left hand.

My time to cross over has come, Two Twists thought even as the crazy white stretched the knife across toward him.

"*Hail* yes!" he whispered softly as he sliced one

135

of Two Twists' braids off. "Scalped me a by-God Injun, 'n' that's a fack!"

Proudly, still grinning affably at the dumb-founded Cheyenne youth, the paleface stuck his 'scalp' in his sash.

"I'm a crazy sumbitch," he informed Two Twists. "Pure-dee crazy 'n' that's a fack!"

Two Twists, who understood not one word of this hair-face gibberish, now said in Cheyenne, "Crazy One! Cut me loose!"

For a long moment the tangle-brain cocked his head like a curious bird. He studied the prisoner, grasping at a meaning that was more in the tone and look the Cheyenne gave him.

"Hear me, Tangle Brain? We Cheyennes can talk to bears, why not crazy whites? You have my braid. Now cut my ropes, and we will be even."

But when the blade glinted cruelly in a stray shaft of sunlight, high over his head, Two Twists chanted his death song.

"Me 'n' the buff," the soft-brain said, "dumb sonsabitches. The Injun, too."

He made a brief, savage sawing motion with his knife, and then Two Twists felt his numb hands slide free.

Quickly, not believing his fortune, Two Twists untied his ankles with clumsy, unfeeling fingers. Then he unlooped the lead line from his horse's bridle. Lame Deer, on the horse in front of him, was too far forward. Two Twists could not risk a sound to alert him.

Sure that a bullet must cancel his life at any moment, he dug his heels into the horse's flanks and jerked the reins hard toward the steep bank beside him.

As he escaped, he heard the crazy white unleash a long laugh behind him.

"The Injun and the buff, all runnin' from the white man! *Hail* yes!"

Chapter Twelve

Unaware yet of the fate of Two Twists and the other hunters, Touch the Sky was forming a grand scheme—a grand scheme whereby the Cheyennes would team up with Uncle Pte to either defeat the hiders or die together.

"Brother," he said to Little Horse, a few sleeps after dramatically scalping and counting coup on Patch Orrick, "one sleep's ride north of the Dunes is a huge, bowl-shaped range. Arrow Keeper pointed it out to me once when we rode to Medicine Lake. Our people never hunt there. Do you know it?"

Little Horse nodded. "It is a dangerous place, according to my clan elders. The ancient High Holy Ones gave it the name Stampede Draw and ordered the Cheyenne people never to hunt there. It is said to be the most dangerous spot on the ancient buffalo trails."

"Dangerous it is, buck, I saw it from a distance. Cover is scarce everywhere on the plains. But Stampede Draw offers not even a hillock or scrub cedar, even the grass grows short. Across this stretch, Arrow Keeper says the herds sniff the Wendigo—he swears they go crazy as dogs in the hot moons when they cross this stretch."

Little Horse was starting to grab hold of his friend's scheme. "Indeed, brother," he said, "not only do they stampede hard, but nothing deters them. Once, when I was still carrying my toy bow, a white wagon train was caught there in a stampede. Not one paleface survived. Their huge bone-shakers were trampled to splinters, not even enough wood left to burn."

"Yes," Touch the Sky said, "that is my point, brother. Not one paleface survived."

Little Horse liked what he was hearing. "But brother, Stampede Draw is well north of this spot. How will we lure the hair-faces?"

" 'Lure,' is the word, buck, I have ears for it. We will lead them just as Wolf Who Hunts Smiling once led a grizzly bear to my cave using bloody bait. The white leader has taken the foolish one with him and ridden out on a mission. But count upon it, they are for us now. Wherever we go, they will follow. So we are going north."

Little Horse watched his friend closely. It seemed a far-fetched plan. And yet, Touch the Sky had turned more and more to 'shaman sensing' in forming his decisions. What seemed foolish or far-fetched in the life of the little day took on different logic in the spirit realm.

"Brother," Little Horse said carefully, knowing it was never proper to talk about holy things too directly, "is there medicine in this plan of yours?"

Touch the Sky nodded.

So did Little Horse. "Then we have no more to discuss, Cheyenne. We will lead these whites to Stampede Draw."

He did not need to add what both bucks were thinking: Their medicine must indeed be strong, the strongest ever. For if the hair-faced hiders could be caught in Stampede Draw, so too could the Cheyenne.

The other three Cheyenne youths, tied tight to horses in front of Two Twists, were unaware of his escape. Nor did they understand what the angry whites were saying when the discovery was made.

"You stupid, shit-for-brains greenhorns!" Myers raged. "Not one swinging peeder saw anything?"

"Ace was ridin' back there," Cecil McGinnis said. "Ask him."

"The hell, 'ask him.' He's a goddamn halfwit. *He* didn't cut him loose. Another Injun musta snuck up and done it."

"Anyhow," McGinnis said, "we still got three."

Myers nodded at that, somewhat mollified. For his purposes, three should do as well as four.

"*Now* we got three. Who knows by the time we reach camp? You, Hoyt, you, Monroe! Herd them other three up to the front. And see if you can keep track of 'em this time."

As Myers turned his horse to resume the lead, he spotted the braid sticking out of Ace's sash.

"What the hell you got there?"

Ace grinned. "Shee-*yit!* Got me a scalp."

Myers studied the half-wit for a long time, suspicion cankering deep in his guts.

"You simple, soft-headed sonofabitch," he said quietly, "I'm loyal to a good man, and you was good in your day. But I've put up with your shit longer than I should have. I don't know if you cut that Innun loose or not. But if I *ever* catch you playing the larks with me, I'll let daylight into your soul."

Ace grinned, baring his broken yellow teeth. "That's a fack, *hail* yes!"

Myers waved him off in disgust. "Move out!" he shouted to the others.

The sun was a dull orange ball on the western horizon by the time Myers and his men reached their camp. The three prisoners, cramped from long hours bent over on horseback, could barely move when they were untied and pulled off their mounts. Patch Orrick, true to his word, was up and about by now, though his ravaged skull was still covered with a linen dressing, now almost as filthy as his chaps.

"There's some lengths of green rawhide in the supply tent," Myers told him. "Fetch enough to stake those three out."

Patch grinned, understanding: Green rawhide was perfect for slow, excruciating torture that made a man scream and beg. As it dried in the hot sun, it shrank remarkably. He had even heard of it shrinking tight enough to cut through a man's limbs and slowly amputate him.

"That tall, English-spoutin' buck and his friends," Myers said, "are in for one helluva show. Hearing these bucks screaming for mercy will take some of the sand out of him and his warriors."

Every moment, as he urged the unfamiliar horse toward the Powder River camp, Two Twists expected a half-ounce buffalo ball to shatter his spine and blow a fist-sized exit hole in his chest.

But as the sun crawled lower and lower without incident, he began to take hope. It would be much better if he could carry the news of his companions' capture directly to Touch the Sky and his band. But Two Twists had no idea where to begin tracking them in these vast ranges.

The only thing for it was to return to the main Cheyenne camp. His companions *had* to be rescued if at all possible. To a Cheyenne, no fate was more terrible than capture by whites, no death more unclean than death by torture at their hands.

He rode through the night, all the next day. By the time he crested the long rise near the confluence of the Powder and Little Powder, he was lightheaded from exhaustion and hunger. His strange horse, iron-shod and rigged white-man style, at first prompted the sentries to raise a wolf howl—the signal that an enemy approached.

Black Elk, Wolf Who Hunts Smiling, and

several other Bull Whip troopers leaped onto the first ponies at hand and rode out to stop him. They recognized him, despite the missing braid and swollen-shut eye where a white hider had kicked him.

"Two Twists!" Black Elk said, lowering his lance. "Little brother, you ride a white man's horse. Good work! Did you also send its owner under?"

They listened attentively while Two Twists described his capture and escape. Chief Gray Thunder and Spotted Tail, leader of the Bowstring troop, rode out to join the group on the slope.

"We must send warriors out to save the hunters," Two Twists concluded. "There cannot be much time."

Chief Gray Thunder held silent, listening to the others to determine how things stood. Black Elk spoke next.

"Two Twists, this thing would be picked up and examined. True, it is a hard thing. Goes Ahead has many relatives in the Bull Whip troop. I know all three young bucks and not one is a shirker. But Cheyenne, only think. Time is not the only consideration. Our tribe is up against it. Even now, as we make words, the marauder Big Tree is leading a war party north."

"And buck," Wolf Who Hunts Smiling said, "have you forgotten that Touch the Sky has already taken a double handful of warriors to fight these hair-faced hiders?"

Now Wolf Who Hunts Smiling caught Gray Thunder's eyes and added, "Or so he says he is fighting them. Clearly they are fighting *us*. I have heard brave tales about how White Man Runs Him grabbed a flag. Pah! A flag does not fight back!"

"Tangle Hair struts about in a white man's hat, Little Horse wears a long knife," Black Elk said. "These could have been gifts, not battle trophies as they claim."

Spotted Tail looked at Wolf Who Hunts Smiling.

"You enjoy speaking against Touch the Sky. Especially when he is not present. Indeed, you will not even respect him enough to use his name. But a thing troubles me, Panther Clan."

"Is there a bone lodged in your throat, Bowstring? Spit this thing out."

"Only this. You speak out a great deal of late, always looking for followers. There was a time when the men of your clan called talkers no better than women. Now, you speak as much as the white fools who leap on stumps to tell their lies. Perhaps, like them, *you* seek power, too?"

"Enough sermonizing," Black Elk said impatiently. "*I* too am one of the men in my cousin's clan. Do you call me a woman, too?"

"Black Elk is far from womanly," Gray Thunder said, "and far from reasonable. Have done with this quarreling, we have enough enemies outside the tribe. Two Twists is right, we *must* do something for the captured hunters. Broken Lance was with Touch the Sky until he was shot in the hip. He will know where to find Touch the Sky's camp. We will send a word-bringer to his band with news of the capture."

Buffalo Hiders

*   *   *

Chief Gray Thunder intended to be fair. But he made one mistake when he selected a word-bringer to take the news to Touch the Sky: He selected a Bull Whip.

The brave's name was Stone Knife of the Wolverine Clan. He was a quiet, some said brooding, warrior who had come under the spell of Wolf Who Hunts Smiling's mesmeric tongue. Some quiet braves were easily influenced by the confident orators among them.

"Have ears, brother," Wolf Who Hunts Smiling told him as Stone Knife cut his pony from the herd and stuffed his legging sash with provisions. "Take your message to White Man Runs Him, just as you have been ordered. Only, leave out one small thing."

Stone Knife squinted his eyes in puzzlement. "What thing, brother?"

"Only this: Two Twists, you know, is one of White Man Runs Him's favorite lackeys. So do not mention that Two Twists has already escaped."

Stone Knife was slow to grasp the use of this. When he did, a brief smile touched his lips. He nodded.

"As you say, brother. I will leave out one small thing."

Chapter Thirteen

"We are up against it, brothers," Full Quiver said, gritting his teeth to counter the unbelievable pain. "Remember that a Cheyenne warrior's worth is determined in the manner of his dying. We may cry out, but we will never beg for mercy!"

"Show these stinking dogs no fear," Lame Deer said. "The more it hurts, the less respect we show. When they bend close to hear us beg, spit in their faces and curse their mothers!"

These brave words took on special worth in light of the three captives' youth. Not one was a blooded warrior, not one had more than 16 winters behind him. All three were staked out naked under a blazing sun. The green-rawhide rope-lengths securing them had been soaked in water to increase the extent of shrinkage as they dried out.

Full Quiver said, "Brothers, where is Two Twists?"

"Either they have killed him," Lame Bear said, "or they are holding him separate from us."

The young brave named Goes Ahead said nothing. The pain was too great and he felt no bravery—only hopelessness and the fear of dying. Already, by mid-morning, the raw-hide bounds had shrunk incredibly tight. The circulation in their arms and legs was cut off, leaving their limbs numb with tingling pain. They had been staked out near red-ant hills, and each youth was covered with angry, swollen bites.

"I wunner what the hell they're sayin'?" Patch Orrick said. He and Sid Myers stood at the perimeter of the buffalo camp, about thirty yards back from the prisoners. The three youths were circled by well-armed guards, with more out in forward positions watching for an attack.

"Don't really matter what they're sayin'," Myers said. "Them three blanket asses're up Shit Creek."

Blood and pus had soaked through Patch's dressing. He was constantly drunk now, whiskey the only antidote for the fiery pain of being scalped.

"They ain't started screaming yet," Patch said. "Want I should help 'em along?"

Myers shook his head. "They'll scream soon enough."

Patch grinned. His eyes were wild and

unfocused now, though still sheening from his urgent need for revenge.

" 'The mills of God grind slowly,' " he quoted, " 'yet they grind exceedingly well.' "

"Here comes Jimmy!" Ace Ludlow said, running up to them. "*Hail* yes!"

The halfbreed scout crossed camp and reined in his big claybank.

"They still out there?" Myers demanded.

"They keep eye on us, you bet. Watch plenty. But the camp, they move it. Go north."

"Moved camp?" Myers couldn't decide whether he was more curious or more disappointed. He didn't want this little show with the prisoners simply to entertain his men, but also the rest of those goddamn Indians. "What the hell for?"

Jimmy was wondering the same thing. He knew damn well those ranges were strong bad medicine for every Plains tribe. And he knew why. But he never volunteered a thing to white men.

"Jimmy doan know, you bet. But plenty buff up north."

Myers nodded, thinking about it. He had done most of his hunting further south, around the Colorado plains.

"Buff," Patch said. "That's why they rode north. They plan on scarin' off another herd."

"Looks that way," Myers said.

"We movin' north, too?"

"It's no skin off our ass if we do. We have to move anyway to find another herd. But Jimmy says they got an eye on us. That means they'll know about the prisoners soon enough if they don't already. Before we move, let's wait a spell. Cheyennes are damn loyal to their own. I got a feeling they'll be back."

Touch the Sky kept one eye on the hiders and the other on the lookout for buffalo birds. He knew the hiders were likewise tracking his position. He was confident they would soon ride north, into Stampede Draw, once they realized the Cheyennes were camped there.

"Brother," Tangle Hair reported, riding in from a scout to the east. "No birds yet. But dust is boiling far out on the horizon. A huge herd is bearing down on us."

"How many sleeps away?"

"Perhaps two. Maybe even less."

Touch the Sky nodded. For a moment he again remembered that feeling of near panic when the buffalo had almost trampled him. Nearby, a dun pony cropped at the grass and stamped impatiently at the flies. She was the sturdy little remount which had replaced his dead mare.

"Buck," Little Horse said, "a thing picks at me. It is good if we can lure the whites into a stampede. But we may succeed only in luring them close for a big kill."

"That is a chance we take, brother."

"Here comes Stone Knife!" Tangle Hair said, pointing. "He rides from the south. He must have tracked us from our last camp."

Stone Knife approached at a long trot, his pony obviously tired. "Touch the Sky!" he called out as soon as he was within hailing distance. "Two Twists and three other hunters have been stolen by the white hiders. The Council of Forty cannot authorize more warriors to leave camp. Therefore, our little brothers' only chance is rescue by your group."

"How do you know this thing?"

"A hunter got away," Stone Knife said, which was not a lie. He simply did not mention that the hunter was Two Twists.

Touch the Sky turned to the rest. "Rig your ponies and prepare to ride."

The Cheyennes pushed their mounts hard for the ride south to the buffalo camp.

The rescue would have been necessary no matter which Cheyennes had been captured. But the seizure of Two Twists gnawed especially hard at Touch the Sky. The loyal youth had not only stood and held like a man during the Kiowa-Comanche attack on their hunt camp one winter ago. He had also ridden with Touch the Sky into the very teeth of Juan Aragon's *Comancheros*, helping to rescue the women and children. He was one of Touch the Sky's first tribal allies besides Little Horse.

Their sister the sun had already given up the sky by the time they rode as close as they dared to the huge camp. But she had already worked her power on the rawhide thongs: the screams which reached their ears proved that.

"Brothers," an angry Tangle Hair said, returning after a quick forward scout of the camp, "it is not only green rawhide causing those screams. The *Mah-ish-ta-shi-da* are making a gruesome ceremony of it. I cannot get in close enough to see faces. But one of our little brothers had lines of black powder laid across his skin and lit. I smelled the stink of it burning! I also saw them piling red-hot rocks on another."

"You cannot see them clearly," Touch the Sky said. "But do you know where they are?"

He nodded. "Perhaps a double stone's throw away from the perimeter. In a straight line from where we stand now."

"Four of them?"

"I could not tell this thing. Several, anyway."

"And the guard?"

"Heavy. They expect us."

"Indeed, it is the reason for this bloody spectacle." Touch the Sky nodded even as another scream from camp made him wince. A chorus of lusty cheers and laughs followed the scream.

"This thing has a bad look to it," Little Horse said. "When have I ever hidden in my tipi when trouble was on the spit? But we cannot possibly assault these dogs. I am down to my last few shells, so are the others low on bullets."

"Bullets, yes," Touch the Sky said. "But we have plenty of black powder."

The rest stared at him in the moonlight. They had marked their faces again with charcoal and they looked almost like carved death masks in the eerie light.

"We have powder," Touch the Sky repeated. "And Little Horse is right. An assault will only get all of us killed. Remember our warrior training. When an attack is out, try a diversion. A diversion that will panic the palefaces. One that gives us enough time to cut our brothers loose and haul them away."

When Touch the Sky pulled several arrows from his quiver, Little Horse caught on. It was the same trick Touch the Sky had used to defeat Sis-ki-dee and his Blackfoot renegades: a Cheyenne invention known as the exploding arrow.

"We will divide into two teams," Touch the Sky said. "The smaller team will be myself, Little Horse, Tangle Hair and Ute Killer. We will move in on foot, locate the powder kegs, and attempt to ignite them. At the first explosion, the second team—mounted—will rush forward and cut our brothers loose. They may not be able to walk or ride, you may have to lash them to ponies. Do not wait for the rest of us, ride north as quickly as possible. We will join you."

It was a desperate plan, but no one questioned it. The screams reaching them from camp meant time was running out and a routine council was out of the question. They would do as their leader said.

They made a total of four exploding arrows, knowing that probably not all of them would work. First, a primer cap was tied to the edge of each arrow. Then a little pouch filled with black powder was tied around the tip of the arrow. While they worked, trying to hurry, more screams came from camp.

Finally the arrows were ready. Each man took one, notching it loosely in his bow. Then began the arduous journey to enter the camp unseen. They had already agreed to fan out on their own, keeping one another in sight. Each would look for powder wagons. At the first good explosion, all would flee.

The sentries were thickest near the prisoners. Others roamed the camp, although they kept deserting their duties to visit the group gathered around the torture victims. So the Cheyennes circled around and entered camp from the opposite side.

Ute Killer was the first to spot a buckboard loaded with the dark shapes of powder kegs. They were grouped closer to the middle of camp since the first Cheyenne raid had sent a wagon into flaming pieces. Ute Killer crouched in the deep grass, took careful aim, launched his arrow. His aim was true. But after a faint sparking, a slight puff of smoke, all was silent— the arrow had detonated, but the powder had failed to catch.

More screams from the opposite side of camp, more ripples of drunken laughter and shouts for more. While Ute Killer low-crawled back to safety, Tangle Hair sighted his arrow on the same buckboard. *Thwap!* Not even a spark. It was a tricky business, lining the primer cap up with the blade. His must have been off by a hair.

Little Horse, a stone's throw to Touch the Sky's right, had sighted a second powder wagon. He rose up on his knees to shoot at it.

Just as Ute Killer, busy watching him, collided with a roaming sentry.

"Innuns!" he shouted. "Up and on the line, we're being attacked!"

The sentry shot Ute Killer point-blank as

Touch the Sky watched, killing him instantly. Touch the Sky saw another sentry spot Little Horse and draw a bead on him. With desperate speed, not even aiming, Touch the Sky launched his fire arrow at the white.

A wet, bursting noise as it struck him in the breast, exploded, blew a spray of meat and muscle and bone and blood. Now everything had come down to the last arrow: Little Horse's. He drew his string taut, released it with a hissing *fwiiip*.

Thwap!

The arrow struck one powder keg in a wagonload. It hit so hard that the fletching quivered long after the impact.

At first, nothing more. Touch the Sky felt his stomach drain cold.

One heartbeat later, the night belonged to chaos.

The resulting explosion was so fierce it flung Touch the Sky and Little Horse to the ground as if they'd been kicked by mules. Touch the Sky glimpsed men and parts of men tumbling through the sky, horses rearing with their eyes all whites, flattened buffalo hides fluttering down like leaves, some of them on fire.

The entire camp lit up like high noon on the Staked Plain. In the ensuing panic, the two Cheyennes leaped to their feet and broke toward their ponies. Out beyond the perimeter, they saw some of their companions fighting guards while others pulled the prisoners up and lashed them to ponies. But they would never survive if they tried to cross camp and join them.

"We have done our duty, Cheyenne!" he called over to Little Horse. "Now hope the others do theirs!"

Dodging bullets and curses, the two warriors escaped into the night.

Chapter Fourteen

Stampede Draw was not dangerous solely because buffalo stampeded hard across it. The real danger lay in the unpredictable *suddenness* of the deadly charge. The entire eastern border was a lush river valley. The herds would graze there quietly, sometimes for days at a time. Then, mysteriously, as if at some unseen signal, the lead bulls would bellow the stampede call.

Even as Touch the Sky, Little Horse, and Tangle Hair raced north to their new camp, a giant herd quietly grazed the hidden valley. In a move born of reckless desperation, the Cheyennes had made camp well out toward the center of the vast Stampede Draw. It was the only way to ensure that the hiders, too, would end up in a vulnerable spot.

Touch the Sky and his companions made

it to camp before the second group. As the night advanced, Uncle Moon climbing slowly toward his zenith, the three of them grew nerve-frazzled with worry. Finally, near dawn, the rest straggled bone-weary into camp, their ponies heaving with exhaustion.

"We have them," the Bowstring trooper named First Son said. "But it was close, brothers. A few Yellow Eyes snapped at our heels and forced us to a merry chase. But though Sun Dance was wounded, none of us was sent under."

"Ute Killer," Touch the Sky said, making the cut-off sign, "was not so fortunate. But our brother died with his knife in his hand."

Touch the Sky was heading toward the rear of the group to check on Two Twists. Dull Knife stopped him.

"The Yellow Eyes have already moved their camp," he said. "We passed them again after shaking off the hiders who chased us."

"Where is Two Twists?" Touch the Sky said, craning his neck to see around Dull Knife's pony. "Is he capable of answering a few questions about these hiders?"

Dull Knife and First Son exchanged uncomfortable glances.

"Brother," First Son said, "we did not find Two Twists with the others. They do not know where he is. Only that, for some reason, the hair-faces are keeping him separate."

This news struck Touch the Sky with the force of a blow. He and Little Horse traded long looks. Little Horse did not like the grim, determined set of his friend's mouth. He had seen it before and knew what it meant.

"Brother," Little Horse said now, "put your foolish ideas back in your parfleche. We do not even know that Two Twists is still alive. Your life is a high price to find out."

"*You* speak of high prices, Cheyenne? You, who leaped in front of a bullet that Seth Carlson meant for me? A bullet that nearly sent you to your funeral scaffold."

Touch the Sky had already made up his mind. It was no one's fault, but Two Twists had been left behind. Soon the whites, too, would be camped out here on the desolate range known as Stampede Draw. Maybe Two Twists *was* dead and beyond help; but then again, maybe he wasn't.

Whichever, Touch the Sky could not risk his braves in another bold raid. A leader could not make that decision. But neither could Touch the Sky leave the fate of Two Twists an unanswered question cankering at him for the rest of his life. Clearly, he decided, he would have to ride back in alone.

For a moment, Touch the Sky felt a cool feather of apprehension tickle the bumps of his spine. He faced east, toward the huge valley that marked the boundary of Stampede Draw. The new sun had just begun to peek out at the sky, streaking it in roseate hues. Again, he remembered how close he had come to being overrun by that buffalo herd.

Little Horse watched his friend. Then he squatted and placed three fingertips lightly against the ground for a long time. Finally he looked at Touch the Sky and shook his head.

"Nothing yet."

Touch the Sky only nodded, saying nothing. But Little Horse was not using the same sense which just now had told Touch the Sky his friend was wrong.

"I swan," Patch Orrick said, gazing all around their new camp. "I seen some god-awful desolate country out here. But *this* has got to be the end of the world! There ain't nothin' out there, not even a damn jackrabbit."

"There's something out there, all right," Sid Myers said grimly. "There's red devils out there. And those red devils're lookin' to scare off all our profits."

They and the hunt-group leader named Cecil McGinnis were unloading tin cases full of .53 caliber buffalo balls—200 to the case. The wagon was full. But the powder wagons were now in much worse shape thanks to this last strike by marauding Cheyennes.

"Hell," McGinnis said, his tone tight with nervousness as he glanced all around them, "I been up agin' redskins plenty in my time. I've hugged with so many tribes I disremember 'zacly how many it was. But this Cheyenne band, why, they're giving us grief six ways to Sunday. Some of the boys, they're all for heading back down to the Colorado ranges."

" 'Some of the boys,' " Myers said with disgust, "gotta squat to piss. Don't matter to me what a bunch of girls with ice in their boots're saying. I'm here to kill buff."

"To kill *Cheyennes*, you mean," McGinnis objected. "I know they done for your family, and I don't blame you for wantin' to plant 'em. But you can't expect us to die just so's you can settle a personal score."

Myers ignored him. Patch, the infection in his scalp wound now rivalling the stink from his scummy chaps, cleared his throat impatiently.

"Long Rifle, you knot-headed sonofabitch! You think *I* ain't got a score to settle with that red nigger? That sumbitch has got my dander tied to his sash! But Cecil here knows shit from apple butter, and he's givin' you the straight. How many times have I pulled your bacon out of the fire? Can't you see it's time to cut our losses and get the hell out? There's something wrong about this place. Something bad wrong. It gives me the willies."

"That's because," Myers repeated, heaving a case of buffalo balls out, "it's no place for men who squat to piss. We got buff to kill. And like I said. A double pouch of gold coins to the swinging peeder that kills that tall Cheyenne buck."

"Gold is as useless as tits on a boar hog," Cecil said, "to a dead man."

While the three whites stood arguing, Myers had kept a curious eye on the scout named Jimmy Longtree. Myers had not given him orders to ride out. Yet the halfbreed had just finished stuffing everything he owned into his leather panniers. Now he swung onto his big claybank.

"Jimmy!" Myers called out. "The hell you going?"

Jimmy reined in his horse. Ever since arriving at Stampede Draw, the claybank had been acting oddly—pawing the earth nervously, constantly glancing toward the east with its ears pricked forward expectantly. The birds, too, Jimmy noticed, were acting strangely.

"Jimmy quit," he announced flatly.

"Quit? Man, you got back wages. I can't pay anybody until we cash in at Red Shale."

"Keep it."

"Damnit, Jimmy, I'll double your wages and throw in that roan mare you're partial to."

This was tempting. Jimmy sat his saddle, thinking about it.

Ace Ludlow wandered up behind the other men. He caught Jimmy's eye and winked. Then he pointed due east and mouthed the words, "Plenty buff." He grinned wickedly when Jimmy's eyes grew big.

"Gotta go, you bet," Jimmy said, spurring his mount. He was suddenly in a hurry to get the hell out of there.

Little Horse now cursed himself for all the lectures he had given Touch the Sky about leadership. For now his brother had left him in charge of the camp—how could he ride out to join him?

Tangle Hair had quickly located the hiders' new camp. Ominously, it was due east, even closer to the beginning of the stampede trail.

Little Horse busied himself readying their defenses. Flank guards had already been sent out. Rifle pits had been dug. The ponies were grazing on long tethers. Now the braves took turns sleeping, exhausted from their ride the night before.

At mid-day the south flanker flashed a mirror signal: friend approaching. Before long an Indian rider appeared in the distance. Little Horse felt his jaw slack open when he recognized Two Twists!

"Little Brother! He has freed you! But where is Touch the Sky?"

Two Twists, looking comically confused with his one missing braid, shook his head. "Brother, I know nothing of Touch the Sky. I have just ridden, after much pleading, from our summer camp to find out about the fate of Full Quiver and the rest."

"Our summer camp?" Little Horse looked even more confused than the younger brave. "Buck, your companions are hurt and tired, but they will live to bounce their children on their knees. Only, tell me this. Are you saying you were not taken prisoner with the other hunters?"

"I was, Little Horse. But I escaped. I returned to camp, and Stone Knife was sent with the word."

Little Horse nodded, suddenly seizing the truth. "Yes, Stone Knife was sent. Stone Knife the Bull Whip. And now, little brother, Touch the Sky has just ridden to a bloody fate. Wolf Who Hunts Smiling and the rest may have gotten their wish this time. If they did, I swear I will use their guts for tipi ropes.

"Come, buck, cut a fresh pony and ride with me. Touch the Sky rode out to save your life. Now you will ride out with me to save his."

Some daylight still remained when Touch the Sky spotted the first cooking fires from the new buffalo camp.

His dun showed no bright markings and was safe from discovery at this distance. He hobbled her at the edge of a buffalo wallow which still held some water. Then he stripped naked and coated his body from head to toe in the dark mud.

He left all weapons behind except for his obsidian-bladed knife. Crouching forward to avoid skylining himself, he slipped quickly through the knee-high grass. A brisk wind rustled the grass and covered the sounds of his movement.

He spotted a picket outpost looming ahead, the shapes of several guards. He swerved wide to the left, spotted another one. Touch the Sky was carefully backtracking, looking for an alternate route, when the world literally dropped out from under him.

Too late, even as he hit the ground hard and the wind was thumped out of him, he realized what had happened. The whites, tired of constant infiltration, had taken a lesson from the red man and dug security pits!

Before he could move, a flaming torch was thrust over the opening in the ground above him. Then a surprised face appeared above him, several more faces, at least four rifle barrels.

He recognized the wild-eyed man with the filthy linen dressing on his head—the same hair face he had scalped.

"Gotcha, blanket ass," Patch Orrick said.

Chapter Fifteen

Even before the sun rose over Stampede Draw, a thick, wet, clinging fog rolled in from the Canadian Plains.

The gray, unbroken mass enveloped everything, including the lush river valley where the huge buffalo herd grazed. But the fog did not deter the lead bulls when, still hours before sunrise, they bellowed the stampede roar.

The fog swirled and drifted, the dark mass of the herd moved under it like a river flowing under a lid of cloudy ice. Shadow-shapes moved up from the valley and out onto the unbroken flats, the ground trembled and vibrated, the air pulsated with a hollow drumming that grew to a roar like a terrible storm blowing in.

Indian legend held that Uncle Pte always sniffed the Wendigo across this stretch and

165

went especially crazy. And indeed, even in the thick fog, the buffalo seemed all white-eyed and agitated. Normally, the sick and the slow were forced to the front. But now, as the bad medicine of Stampede Draw worked its spell, the buffalo deserted all custom. One by one, they trampled their own to death.

Like a monstrous, unstoppable juggernaut, the herd roared out across the Plains, a great, shaggy death machine.

Sid Myers figured the Wheel of Fortune had finally taken an upturn for him.

Every hider in camp knew by now who had literally fallen into their hands—the tall, English-speaking Cheyenne buck who led the warriors currently harassing them. Already, the atmosphere in camp was noticeably improved.

The Great Red Bogey had been exposed for what he was—a helpless, naked savage covered with mud, his face childishly streaked black. A savage foolish enough to attack a camp by himself armed with nothing but a bone-handled knife. A savage who would die hard in front of all the men—die the same way Myers' family had died at Cheyenne hands.

By Myers' strict order, Touch the Sky was not beaten or tortured. Myers wanted him fully conscious and aware for his execution. He was taken to the center of camp and trussed tight to the tongue of a wagon. By the time the morning sun began burning off the thick fog, curious men had gathered around him. Patch Orrick was among them.

"Hell," said one, "he ain't so big now, is he?"

"You untie him, Jeb," somebody joked, "and I'll wager he gets bigger!"

"*Hail*, yes!" said the skinny, crazy-by-thunder white man who had been staring at Touch the Sky as if he were a pink elephant. He pulled the braid from his sash and dangled it in front of the prisoner. "Got me a Injun scalp, 'n' that's a fack!"

The men roared with laughter while Touch the Sky held his face impassive. So far he had seen no sign of Two Twists. But he recognized the distinctive pattern of his young friend's braid. Had they already killed him, then?

"Where's *my* scalp, you stinkin', flea-bit blanket ass?"

Touch the Sky couldn't turn his head away when the wild-eyed white man, reeking of alcohol and filth, squatted close to him. A greenish discharge oozed through his head dressing.

"I asked you where's my dander, buck?"

"It's not on your head any more, is it, cockroach?" Touch the Sky said in English.

The men roared with laughter even as Patch turned livid. He curled his big hands into fists. But suddenly Sid Myers emerged from the thinning fog like a wraith. The big man carried one of the curved knives used for removing buffalo hides.

"He took your scalp," Myers said. "Now take his hide. And take it off *slow*."

Silence fell over the huge circle of men. They had crowded even closer to see through the fog.

"I don't know, Sid," Cecil McGinnis finally said. "Course he's got to die, he killed white men. But ain't skinning him goin' a little too far? By God, he's got starch in him, Innun or no. He deserves a better death."

Several of the men spoke up in favor of this. But Myers was implacable.

"My wife and six-year-old boy deserved better, too! Cheyennes cut their eyelids off and left them under the summer sun all day. Can you goddamn imagine what that musta felt like, their eyes frying in their skulls? But that wasn't enough. When them red vermin was done cuttin' and carvin' on them, you couldn't even tell what sex they was!"

"Hell, that's rough, all right," McGinnis said quietly. "But, Sid, them was Southern Cheyenne. Renegade Dog Soldiers at that, all likkered up. This here is a Northern Cheyenne. They're—"

"Shut your gob, Cecil," Patch said. "You Injun-lovin' shitheel! Shut your gob. That red varmint skinned me. Now I'm gunna by God skin *him!* Any squeamish sonofabitch ain't got the stomach for it can turn his head."

Patch took the curved skinning knife from his boss. Touch the Sky, his face defiant, met the man's fervent eyes boldly.

"You're a coward and a pig's afterbirth," he said. "I counted coup on you, and I took your hair. I want every man here to remember Touch the Sky of the Northern *Shaiyena*, a warrior and a fighting Cheyenne. Now, white pig, make your coward's cut. Cut deep, cut hard, and *see* if this Cheyenne begs for mercy!"

"Pretty speech, red nigger. But you *will* beg."

Patch leaned forward. Touch the Sky felt the cold steel touch his skin—and then he felt something else.

The ground trembling.

Everyone had fallen silent as Patch began to make his cut. Now they all heard it: a steady rumble, building in the east. But the fog still lay thick in that direction, and nothing could be seen beyond the edge of camp.

The ground trembled a little harder, the air began to pulsate, and then somebody screamed the single word that struck bone-numbing panic into 200 men:

"Stampede!"

Every man, including Patch Orrick and Sid Myers, immediately forgot about the Cheyennes and everything else except saving his own hide. Men broke for the rope corral, leaving all their gear behind.

The ground shook harder, the noise built like an approaching avalanche. Uselessly, Touch the Sky struggled against his ropes. Still, he couldn't see anything in the fog.

Until Little Horse and Two Twists suddenly materialized out of it, leading his dun pony!

"Brother, Uncle Pte is on the warpath!" Little Horse greeted him. He leaped off his pony, knelt to slice through his friend's ropes. "Now let us make tracks and hope this is not our day to die!"

Touch the Sky grabbed a handful of mane and swung up onto his mount. The three Cheyennes raced across camp, leaping obstacles, headed for

169

the far side of camp away from the direction of the stampede. But the noise seemed to come from all around them now.

Against the rumbling din, the sharp crack of a pistol. Touch the Sky glanced to his right through swirling mist: Myers was drawing another bead on him with his Navy Colt.

Little Horse uttered the war cry and slid his stolen saber from his sash. He leaped his ginger, swung the saber in a wide arc, and deftly severed Myers' head clean from his shoulders. It rolled and bounced through the grass, eyes wide open and staring, even as the headless body took several steps, blood splashing in jets from the neck.

The body flopped down and Little Horse threw the bloody saber on top of it. "There, hair face! I have only been waiting for a chance to give the long knife back!"

But this triumph was muted by the reality of their danger. The stampede was now so close that Touch the Sky felt the ground shifting under him like a canoe on rough water.

They heard screams from just beyond the edge of camp. Then whites, mounted now, were returning to camp in a panic.

"Jesus, I just saw Bill get trampled! We're surrounded!" one of them shouted. "There's no way out!"

And then, just as Touch the Sky was wondering why Uncle Pte had not overrun the camp itself, the stampede abruptly halted.

It grew quiet as death. Every man in camp could hear the buffalo out there. They ringed the entire camp, and now they were waiting.

But waiting for what?

"Easy, boys," Patch Orrick's voice called slow and soft out of the nearby fog. "Easy now. Stay frosty and don't make no sudden, loud noises. There's a million or more buff out there. The camp and all the white man's stink has got 'em spooked. If we keep quietlike, they'll eventually go around us."

A long silence after he fell quiet. Touch the Sky could hear Uncle Pte out there in the damp fog. Breathing, stamping the ground, gathering for the slightest excuse to make another mad charge.

"Shee-*yit!*" said a voice in Touch the Sky's ear, making him flinch hard. "Let ol' Ace show you a trick. You think *I'm* dumb? Watch the buff."

The tangle-brained white man grinned affably at the dumbfounded Indians. He held a Volcanic repeating rifle, though it wasn't aimed at them. Two Twists, uncertain, raised his rifle, but Touch the Sky stopped him with a hand on his arm.

"Leave it alone, little brother," he whispered. "The High Holy Ones are in on this thing."

Ace Ludlow loosed a fine imitation of a buffalo calf bawling in distress. Just as he had learned from watching Patch Orrick.

"Oh, Jesus Katy Christ! *Goddamn* it, Ace!" Orrick's voice pleaded out of the fog. "*Don't* do it, you simple shit, *please!*"

Again Ace bawled like a calf in misery. Moments later, a buffalo cow plodded into camp looking for the young one.

"*Hail*, yes!" Ace said gleefully, dropping the cow with one loud shot that was greatly amplified in the damp fog. "Gonna get me a juicy sumbitchen liver!"

That shot unleashed madness and mayhem and hell-spawned terror as the vast herd suddenly stampeded through the camp.

Touch the Sky flashed a desperate signal to his friends, and all three leaped under a loaded wagon. Now a huge, dark wall of shaggy fur exploded through the camp. Touch the Sky saw Patch Orrick emerge from the mist, his face a frozen mask of fear. A heartbeat later, he went down screaming under thousands of pounding hooves.

Now the entire camp disappeared in a crazy, swirling, bellowing inferno. Men screamed, horses nickered, wagons and hide-presses and packs of buffalo hides were crushed and scattered. Touch the Sky felt the wagon above them start to shudder and heave. A moment later it shattered completely, and the Indians were lucky not to be crushed under the load as they scrambled out from under it. But death seemed certain now.

"Sing the death song, brothers!" Little Horse shouted in their ears, though it sounded like a whisper in the din.

But Touch the Sky, his thinking more and more shaped by Arrow Keeper's shaman training, stepped directly into the swirling confusion. He placed one hand on his medicine pouch to give his words special magic.

"Uncle Pte!" he shouted. "We are your allies

in the struggle for life! Uncle Pte, the fate of the buffalo is the fate of the red man! Though our days are numbered, let us live longer that *you* may live longer!"

For the rest of their lives all three Cheyennes would remember what happened next. Uncle Pte, in a clear effort to avoid them, swerved wide and passed them in a double column.

Many of the hiders were not so fortunate.

Some had miraculously escaped, their horses deftly joining the stampede until they could break free. But most now littered the annihilated camp, some trampled so badly they were unrecognizable as human. It was a sad sight, and not one Cheyenne rejoiced in it. But neither could they forget their feelings when they discovered the buffalo boneyard left by these hiders who killed Indians almost as casually as they slaughtered buffalo.

They spent some time chasing down their mounts. When they returned, they discovered one white survivor: Ace Ludlow. The feeble-brain wandered the ruined camp aimlessly, muttering to himself.

The Cheyennes left him, after making sure he was provisioned for many days. Insane whites had an odd status with Indians. They were to be avoided, of course, but also respected and cared for, as one would care for a helpless child. *Never* could one be deliberately hurt or killed. Such a violation of the warrior code would cost a man his coup feathers for life.

"Brothers," Little Horse said as they began

the ride to join their companions at camp. "We must return here with travois before we ride back to Gray Thunder's camp. Plenty of rifles and supplies escaped damage. We will take them back, our people need them. When the tribe learns how completely the hiders have been destroyed, the rumors against you must cease."

But Touch the Sky, despite the weary elation of this victory for Uncle Pte, knew the rumors and plots would *never* cease. Not as long as his tribal enemies lived. Look how Wolf Who Hunts Smiling's most recent treachery had nearly killed him.

"Shee-*yit!*" Ace shouted behind them. When they turned, he waved good-bye to them. "Me 'n' the buff, dumb sonsabitches. *Hail* yes!"

"What is the soft-brain saying?" Two Twists asked.

Touch the Sky grinned. "Some would say he speaks peyote talk. But, brothers, he is only telling us that Uncle Pte is *his* friend, too."

CHEYENNE

JUDD COLE

Born Indian, raised white, Touch the Sky swears he'll die a free man. Don't miss one exciting adventure as the young brave searches for a world he can call his own.

#1: Arrow Keeper.
__3312-7 $3.50 US/$4.50 CAN

#2: Death Chant.
__3337-2 $3.50 US/$4.50 CAN

#3: Renegade Justice.
__3385-2 $3.50 US/$4.50 CAN

#4: Vision Quest.
__3411-5 $3.50 US/$4.50 CAN

Judd Cole
Follow the adventures of Touch the Sky as he searches for a world he can call his own!

#5: Blood on the Plains. When one of Touch the Sky's white friends suddenly appears, he brings with him a murderous enemy—the rivermen who employ him are really greedy land-grabbers out to steal the Indian's hunting grounds. If the young brave cannot convince his tribe that they are in danger, the swindlers will soak the ground with innocent blood.

_3441-7 $3.50 US/$4.50 CAN

#6: Comanche Raid. When a band of Comanche attack Touch the Sky's tribe, the silence of the prairie is shattered by the cries of the dead and dying. If Touch the Sky and the Cheyenne braves can't fend off the vicious war party, they will be slaughtered like the mighty beasts of the plains.

_3478-6 $3.50 US/$4.50 CAN

#7: Comancheros. When a notorious slave trader captures their women and children, Touch the Sky and his brother warriors race to save them so their glorious past won't fade into a bleak and hopeless future.

_3496-4 $3.50 US/$4.50 CAN

LEISURE BOOKS
ATTN: Order Department
276 5th Avenue, New York, NY 10001

Please add $1.50 for shipping and handling for the first book and $.35 for each book thereafter. PA., N.Y.S. and N.Y.C. residents, please add appropriate sales tax. No cash, stamps, or C.O.D.s. All orders shipped within 6 weeks via postal service book rate. Canadian orders require $2.00 extra postage and must be paid in U.S. dollars through a U.S. banking facility.

Name _____

Address _____

City _____ State _____ Zip _____

I have enclosed $_____in payment for the checked book(s). Payment <u>must</u> accompany all orders.☐ Please send a free catalog.